ELEMENTARY SCHOOL:
WITS AND TWITS

ACKNOWLEDGMENTS

*I wish to thank all those in my personal
life who made this book possible.*

MR. NICK PRODUCTIONS, LLC
©2018 by Mr. Nick Productions, LLC

Edited by my longtime friend and editor/writer,
Marilyn Milow Francis – Thank you

Front cover art – Patrick Jankowski
Book layout – Kristy Klein | seeingistudio.com

Photo of hapless fourth grader – Anonymous
Published by Mr. Nick Productions, LLC ©2018

ISBN: 978-0-692-10167-4

Dedication

To my elementary school, that not only *schooled* me, but eventually let me out to continue into seventh grade, and beyond. Thank you, I think.

Foreword

Those seven years (K-6) in elementary school weren't wasted, were they? They were the best seven years of my life, right? It's hard to tell; it could have gone either way.

The ultimate prequel, or is it? I decided to rattle my pea brain and dust off the cobwebs of my gray matter to go deep into the vault and mine some outrageous and sadly funny stories from my elementary school education. Why go so far back, just to make people cringe and laugh? I don't know. In addition to my comedic books already in print, I thought a humorous stroll down an ancient and twisted memory lane would bring some fresh levity to my former classmates and others who might enjoy my reminiscences. It wasn't all anguish and nervousness, although I did bite my fingernails well into adulthood. Hopefully this book will rekindle and expose some of that elementary school anxiety AND fun that I thought was appropriate to elucidate. Although loosely based on my memory and interpretation of actual events, this book is "technically" fictional. It is a book of humor and should be taken as such. There is no malicious intent; the only intent is to entertain!

Dr. I. Mayputz

TABLE OF CONTENTS

KINDERGARTEN

FIRST GRADE

SECOND GRADE

THIRD GRADE

FOURTH GRADE

FIFTH GRADE

SIXTH GRADE

Introduction

This book is about a slightly fictionalized account of my life in elementary school, inspired by actual events. Embellishments of strange happenings were unnecessary because human foibles ran rampant. However, most names and places have been changed so as not to embarrass the guilty, inept and downright scurvy. The stories are retold in a series of vignettes which best captured my mood at the time. Those long-ago times were filled with tears, jeers and soiled underwear, not to mention the puddles of urine and vomit during the early years. Those who kept their wits about themselves usually survived and thrived; those who were twits, not so much. Our parents and teachers wanted us to learn and prosper; we just desired to play, eat lunch, defecate and go home – to play some more. I wanted to relive those vapid memories, some good, some bad, and to entertain you in the process. Perhaps you will laugh along with me. Maybe at me, as well!

Enjoy.

Dr. I. Mayputz

KINDERGARTEN

1

School 90

I have a confession to make. Although the following initial vignettes will showcase my sometime malfunctional early life, I actually had a slight advantage over my perceived competitive compatriots, at least at the beginning, such as in kindergarten. I was born in a large city in western New York State, to Estonian immigrant parents that had met and married in the U.S. My father was educated stateside, as a civil engineer, after dropping out of art school. Although a talented artist from his home country, traditional art was no longer in vogue in America by the late '50s. If you weren't a controversial Andy Warhol clone or Picasso adherent, there were no good paying jobs available. So, begrudgingly and sadly, he quit the bizarre, artsy-fartsy world, became educated as a *menschy* civil engineer and glumly went to work. My mother was a stay-at-home mom, at the time. We lived in an upstairs apartment in a small urban house that we three shared with my paternal grandparents, also relatively recent immigrants. It was a strained and stressful relationship between the extended kinsfolk with domineering male Chieftains and perceived as docile, female Indians, and me.

However, lots of people in my neighborhood had the same familial "dysfunctional" dynamics but they chose to live like that, to save money and keep things in the "family," so to speak. Our immediate street was immaculate and composed mainly of eastern European and Slavic families, all jumbled together, living in nearly touching homes on narrow and congested streets. Every Sunday afternoon the menfolk would mow their patches of lawn with manual, push reel mowers, trim the hedges, and wash their Oldsmobiles, Buicks and Chevys. Each spoke his/her own language at home and broken English out in the streets. The native born youngsters (like me) had no accents, of course, and were real Americans, so we naively thought. Hey, we all religiously watched Captain Kangaroo, Popeye, The Three Stooges and Looney Tunes on TV. We kind of looked the same, had similar haircuts, and felt comfortable and safe. In addition, there were adjacent streets that were TRULY homogenous. There was the German town, Little Italy, the Irish zone, the Chinese section, the Polish district, etc. Ours was more of a hodgepodge of Europeans, but we all got along. ALL the men worked, while the mostly kerchiefed women gossiped rancorously, while hanging laundry, across fences separating the miniscule backyards. The huge Broadway indoor/outdoor market attracted mainly the new immigrants, with food and deli selections that would be considered "foreign" to most locals. I loved going there. Fresh herring from the fishmonger, newly ground Polish sausage, sweets from Latvia, bread so tasty it didn't need butter. Those were the days. We were all Christian by denomination and would dutifully meander to our own respective churches on most Sundays mornings. However, it was more of a social gathering than fire and brimstone, as the immigrants fiercely tried to keep their cultures and languages alive, for as long as possible. Church sermons were in the mother tongue; eligible and marriageable parishioners probably eyeballed each other for dating and mating purposes. That's how things were and, most likely, going to be in my life as well. However, by 1963 things in my household started to change. My mom had taken it upon herself to homeschool me and I could read at an early age. Then, while other mothers were still immersed in their cloistered cultures, mine took a brave step and enrolled me that fall into a bona fide, coed preschool half-day program at the elementary school called School 90, which was directly across the street from our house. This was a blasphemous move, however. There would be typical American white kids present, and only English would be spoken. Holy Hell! But I fit in fine and recognized a few of my street friends there as well. Miss Silsky was my extremely attractive teacher. She was no babooshka. Long brown hair, big brown eyes, tall, svelte, a silky voice and leather boots up to her knees. How could you not fall in love with her as a three-year-old? I was loving school, socializing well with those "real Americans," and not getting any knots in my shoelaces. Miss Silsky had a special fork she used to untie stubborn knots with. I think some boys purposely tied knots just to have the lovely teacher fondle their feet while trying to undo the mess they made. We also learned how to socialize, how to figure out simple problems and skill games, and continued to read, read and read. I would be more than ready for kindergarten, Miss S. assured my mom, and it turned out to be true. However, about this time there were grumblings at my house. My paternal grandmother had passed away, my grandfather was restless, and my father was unhappy with his job. Things became quickly unsettled just as I was happily settling into life. My previously verbose, confident and manly dad needed a change. To make a long story shorter, my mom found an advertisement in a local newspaper about an available professorship at a junior Ag and Tech college in upstate New York. On a whim, my pop applied, drove through a blinding snowstorm in his '54 rear wheel drive Nash Rambler for an interview, but failed to secure the position. However, the benevolent university then directed him to another two-year college slightly farther south, that had a similar vacant and tenured position available and, this one he nailed. He was hired as an assistant professor of civil engineering, for the spring semester, and enthusiastically phoned my mother with the "good" news. But he was six hours away from home, in the boonies, with deer, bears, wolves and coyotes lurking along the barren roadways. He was from the city. Where was he now? Back on a rural farm in Estonia? Suddenly my mom was afraid, as she told me later. Were there any churches in town? Was there a school for little Izzy? Where would we live? All of those questions, and more, my pop couldn't answer at the time. He had taken a big chance and a big pay cut to become an untested and greenhorn professor but the bennies were great and a pension was in store if you taught for at least 20 years. There was one traffic light in the small village, one motel, a hospital, a public high school with a ritzy sounding name, one police officer, a county sheriff, and one jail cell. He was warned by the hiring vice dean of academic affairs that the "inbred" townspeople were on the rough side and didn't relish mingling with the *intellectual* and diverse college community up on the hill. And what was up with the purple-colored soil that protruded among the snow piles in town? He phoned my mom once more and they made up their minds to move. My grandpa was

sad, my mom excited, and me? What had just happened?
Welcome to Bumfuck, N.Y., bucko, where the dirt was
weird, the suspicious natives were even weirder, and where
I would grow up. Who knew?

2

Trikes and Fire Trucks

Being the firstborn and only child thus far, I handsomely raked it in when my birthday rolled around. Turning three proved to be no exception. Among the many toys I received that October were a handsome tricycle and a pedal-driven, all metal, fire truck with tiny yellow ladders, a working bell and squeezable horn. I was in heaven. My city-living driveway was miniscule but perfect for me. I was a tiny tyke, remember? I rode my trike and fire truck daily until the snow flew. Neighborhood kids would come over and pretend to play with me, only to ride my prize possessions. I liked the adulation, but it was for my toys, not me. My mom would readily evict them if she saw me just standing there being ignored, watching "friends" play with MY stuff. Not everyone had TWO rubber-wheeled vehicles at such a young age. The tricycle was eventually given to a relative, but the fire truck remained in my family until my baby sister outgrew it, years after we had moved away from the city and into the country. She had loved it as much as I had. The wheels fell off, the body rusted out, and the wooden ladders were long gone when my father finally trashed it. During my last year of high school, I remember my driver education instructor being somewhat stupefied at my excellent parallel parking and backing up skills while learning how to drive. On numerous occasions he would accuse me of already knowing how to operate an automobile and berate me for it. He didn't like being duped by a wise-ass student looking for an easy A, especially a senior. Finally, I relented and told him and the other students present that I learned how to drive thanks to my fire truck, long ago. You see, I didn't just pedal push that toy car around. Even as a toddler, I set up small cones, backed it up, and parallel parked it one-handed, just like I was doing in his class. Mr. K. just stared at me in disbelief before thinking hard about what I had said. I could see the wheels turning as a grin broke over his face. He never said another word to me as I expertly and one-handedly maneuvered the driver ed's light blue, four-door Pontiac Bonneville forwards and backwards. I even received the driver education award at graduation. All that because of a little red fire engine and a three-year-old that loved to drive.

3

Zoo or Nursing Home?

The one-eyed lion, the one-eared polar bear, the one-legged penguin, the one-tusked male walrus. Come on, it was true I tell you. The local zoo was close by and most weekends found my mom, pop and me on a quick jaunt through it. Why not? What else could you do on a Saturday, in the crowded city, with a three-year-old? It was almost free and I got to see a multitude of banged up animals up close for at least an hour, before we headed home. We usually arrived at feeding time, and watched the caged and mangy relics of once noble beasts devour their meaty vittles. I threw candy to the bears even though you weren't supposed to. Everyone else did; what did I know at that age? Plus I had my token hot dog and ice cream bar, which I looked forward to eating. Many, many years later, on a planned vacation trip to Niagara Falls, my family convinced me to revisit the "zoo," after hearing years of insulting comments about it from me. Okay, then. I would show my children the hellhole and repository for disabled creatures, large and small. THEY wanted to witness and laugh at the crapped-up *animules*, firsthand. I parked the minivan, started chuckling, paid the exorbitant entrance fees and we entered. I suddenly realized that the zoo of yesteryear was merely on a low-budget holding pattern with a dilapidated infrastructure and obviously deranged, near death animals. The zoo of the early sixties was a shameful mess; the updated version, that we were now in, was a pristine "animal garden" with fully functional and lively carnivores as well as content looking megavegetarians. And, all the critters had legs, paws and fins! I was shocked. My family called me a liar as I stared bug-eyed at the wonderful scene in front of me. No amount of excuses mollified my wife and kids. Nevertheless, it was a pleasure to stroll through the beautiful enclosures with my own family, buy them hot dogs and then the obligatory ice cream bars. It was well worth the price of admission. What a difference four decades made.

4

The Escape

It was the Beverly Hillbillies' moving experience, but in reverse. Although relatively recent immigrants, my old-world folks had picked up enough big city savvy to MAKE it, regardless where that place was. It would have been hard to *punk* them back then. They were young, ready for an unexpected homesteading adventure, and eager to challenge themselves in a new frontier, albeit a possibly hostile one. Even if there had been Indians in the picture, they still would have gone. But no, they were only moving across the state to a miniscule village that had one popular "greasy spoon" diner and a primitive party-line telephone system. So, things were not so dire, after all. Or, were they? Housing, food, education, medical treatment, and an orthodox church were on the "list" when we arrived in town on a Saturday in early February for an exploratory visit, in early '64. My mother was pregnant with my baby sister, and needed comfort and rest. Of course they lodged in the only motel in town, which was next to the rural hospital. Mom thought the mattress was stuffed with manure, but then she noticed that a window in their room had been left open. Ah, FRESH country air!

But at least now they knew there was a medical facility present, which meant doctors, nurses, and at least a drugstore, somewhere. And look, there was a magnificently perched, old-style, Roman-columned high school up on the hill across from the hospital. My folks crossed two things off their list. Next was housing. The college had provided my dad with a very incomplete and cursory list of potentially available rental situations. Being a small town with few streets, my pop whizzed the car around and within two hours had talked to many townies on that list, and even to their nosy neighbors, about renting to us. No dice. Why? The knock on the door was perfect and my handsome father got smiled at, but every time he opened his accent laden pie hole, the homeowner would recoil. Who the hell were these olive-skinned people? My old man sounded like those despicable "Soviets" that were constantly mentioned on TV What? The U.S.S.R., baby! The "Russians" were invading a one-horse town. And no matter how much my father pleaded and tried to convince the locals that he was indeed a college professor, was married and had a son, it was the same old answer. Outsiders, especially those damn "Russkies," were not welcome. This was the height of the Cold War, remember? What if we had been sent by the Kremlin disguised as "intelligence moles?" Holy shit. No one wanted to harbor spies. When my father mentioned the word Estonia to one owner/renter, it sounded like he said he was stoned and the homeowner swore at him and slammed the door in his face. It had been a bad day, thus far. We had one last home to check out and it did not look promising from the outside. It was hopelessly small, with weathered blue clapboards and a new Cadillac parked in the driveway. And it had a rental apartment? How? However, before he steeled himself for yet another rejection, pop drove us to the other diner in town, at the foot of the college, one that he was told was more open-minded toward strangers. College students frequented that place so the owners saw their fair share of strangeness. We were politely served lunch, paid up, used the facilities, and quickly went back to that last potential rental on the list. It had started snowing now and my dad had an idea. All three of us would approach the would-be renter and plead our case in unison. Maybe he/she would take pity on a pitiful looking boy? Retired math teacher Mrs. Arbuckle opened the door and immediately invited us in, out of the snowy sleet. This time my mom spoke up first, with me playing the role of the woebegone waif. Mr. Arbuckle came by, sized us up, listened to our spiel, showed us the puny two-bedroom apartment upstairs, and shook hands with my old man. There was no lease. Just a gentleman's agreement for a year. We had a place to live and could move in at any time. $60 per month included everything, even the phone service. I think my mother started to cry in gratitude. But there was no "real" food market in town. At least not the gigantic kind she was used to. Farmer's markets and organic foodstuffs were in our distant future unless you lived on a farm. Those were plentiful; seemingly all around us. But for we proper village dwellers though, there were two "supermarkets" on Main Street, Grand Union and Victory, as well as a few mom-and-pop shops. Oh, there was a failing butcher in town as well. And it wasn't the local dentist! Anyway, the "list" was tossed and we drove to the elementary school up the hill from the majestic high school, parked the car and admired the Catskills from our high vantage point. My artistic father remarked that he had never seen such beauty in all his life. The air was clean, there was no city noise, and the snow-covered trees resembled scenes on a postcard. My mom mumbled that she was glad to get out from under the dictatorial thumb of her father-in-law, who remained behind in the city. She also smiled and chuckled that of the ten churches they had passed by, none were Christian Orthodox. The village believers were Methodists, Episcopalians, Catholics, Baptists, Lutherans, Evangelicals, Presbyterians, and Christian Scientists. Oh, well. I had already been baptized Estonian Orthodox, so I was good to go. No church, no problem. My parents tended to lean toward the agnostic anyway, so no one panicked. I spoke next. "I love this place," I remember saying out loud. Did I though? Was I merely parroting my parents' optimistic utterings to fit in? I would be leaving friends, Miss Silsky and my home, to live in this silent and prejudiced township. But as my parents seemed thrilled I didn't buck the trend. The next week found us moving in for real, with old Mr. Arbuckle helping us unload the moving truck of our meager possessions. I had quit preschool and began homeschooling again with my mom. She joined the V.I.S. (Village Improvement Society) to try to fit into her new turf. They rubbed elbows on Saturdays, in alternating homes. There, she met many like her; misfits trying to adapt to Americana and small village dictums. Our family wasn't the only one subjected to animosity and bias by the ruling gentry. The Korean war brides of white locals also felt the brunt of stigmatization. Their "ethnic looking" children were like me: American but different. But she managed to befriend some "white" residents that were not only kind to her but ended up becoming lifelong friends of our family. My dad was quickly accepted into the "college convent" as a brilliant but hard-to-understand young professor. His intelligence superseded any qualms about his lack of adequate enunciation or teaching expertise and he rapidly got the hang of things. And he started to love his new job. That's what he told us nightly, anyway. It must have been true because he retired as the Chairman of the Engineering Department after a thirty-plus year stint. My mom also retired from the same college as a long-tenured French and Spanish professor. How did that happen, to a hard-core housewife, no less? I won't go into it now. Suffice it to say that my conservative parents took it upon themselves to leave the "safety" of a multicultural block, a foreigner's state of mind, physically extricate themselves and me from a congested, immigrant-infused city, and move into the "wilderness" on a wing and a prayer. Nevertheless, it seemed to have worked out. I'm sure it extended both of their lives with decreased stress due in part to slowed-down village living. And me? My mom was at home at the time and my pop was in his insulated cocoon of collegial thinkers. I would bear the proverbial cross as a newbie kindergartner in a new school with the local yokel spawn. Gone were my carefree days with the city *boyz* that understood me in a variety of languages. Gone was my small patch of grass and backyard pear tree. Gone was Miss Silsky and School 90. And gone was my small piece of mind. But my sister had already been hatched in the village hospital in May and things became crowded in that smallish apartment by the time I was ready for my scholastic endeavors. Kindergarten would commence at the very end of summer and I would be there, on schedule. Was I ready? Yes. Was I afraid? You bet.

5

Another Mouth in the House

My *infank* (spelling and pronunciation courtesy of Popeye) sister technically began kindergarten with me in the late autumn of 1964. Well, she rode in my mother's arms as we strode into the brand-new elementary school building that drizzly and chilly fall morning, on my first day. I didn't take the bus because I was nervous and my mom knew it. I just wanted to get to school on time and get on with things, especially on the introductory day. It wasn't my first time there, however. We three had come earlier in the week for the required *disorientation day*, complete with an assembly, featuring teachers and the reigning educational dignitaries, followed by lunch and a cursory tour of my new school. I was now a full-time student and my mom should have gotten a break. Not so fast, though. Now we had another mouth to feed, another yowling, howling, baby human in our puny rental apartment on Clinton Street. My sister! I was five years her senior and lorded it over her; the BIG brother. However, as she grew, it became sort of fun to have her as a foil. She was now someone to tease, to play with, and even to converse with, on a limited basis that is. But even as a crawler and then toddler, she displayed annoying signs of higher intelligence. Darn it. And I mistakenly thought that I was Top Cat (an old Hanna-Barbera cartoon series in the early sixties) in the household. It quickly became obvious that she was quick-witted, precocious and had a sense of humor at an early age. I confess to having had fleeting feelings of inadequacy and thoughts of being supplanted by her as the new and improved model child in the house. It didn't happen. Honestly speaking though, we almost became equals, only my gender's physicality and older age kept me in a slightly superior hierarchal position. Anyway, things got crowded in a hurry at our tiny living quarters and we had to move. We had no choice. So we moved up the street, to a small rental house, and picked up where we left off in life.

6

The First Day of School

Well, this was it. The moment of dread, trepidation and education, all rolled into one. My mom, baby sister and I had already visited that *penal* place, in order for me to become familiarized with the joint. Now it was time to begin my official public school learning process. The elementary school building was very new, the cornerstone read 1962; I was officially a kindergartner that fall. Was I ready? Most likely. I had a brief introduction to a classroom setting in preschool, the year prior. I felt prepared, plus I was not in a position to protest. Resistance was futile. I let go of my mother's hand, looked at my sister one last time, and entered the world of sanctioned scholarship. Book bag, pencils and paltry supplies, a bagged lunch and a smock for painting; I was ready. Miss N. welcomed each student and patted we younglings on the head as we entered her classroom one by one. I looked up at her and smiled, then looked straight ahead and panicked. In front of me was an ocean of pale faces, fair hair and mostly blue eyes. After a summer of practically living outdoors and gaining a great tan and, being genetically predisposed, I looked like Mowgli the

Jungle Boy, misplaced in a jungle of "white" people. With black hair in a bowl cut and an olive skin tone, the local kids in that class stared back at me. Was it their first encounter with a "colored" child? In my western New York city of birth, I blended in beautifully with the other brown-skinned, brown-eyed and black-haired children of eastern European immigrants. Not so here. Were they albinos? At least they spoke English, which I understood perfectly. I swallowed hard and proceeded to interact that first morning. You know, meet and greet. There were some questions asked of me, there were some answers given, there were some comments made. Lots of the children resembled one another, and seemed to know each other. I quickly figured out that they must be related in some way, and I was right. Much later did it dawn on me that while the last names changed, the genetic stock was basically the same for generations. The locals all bred with each other, much like the cattle they were farming, producing brood after brood of kindred kin. Okay, there were a few miscolored misfits like me thrown in. But they were also locals and already known to the mostly tow-headed, motley crew in my class. I was the true outsider and needed to fit in as best as I could in a hurry. One boy, Nicky Z., immediately ran to me, sized me up, and said a few humorous things about my appearance. He thought he was a funnyman; I didn't laugh at his jokes, but other kids did. I fancied MYSELF as a live wire, and here was an immediate competitor for class clown status and supremacy. Well at least I also thought of myself as being smart. However, that Z. character was intelligent too, darn it. Eventually I bested him in both categories but not before exchanging many, many barbs and zingers with him. Plus I was a much better athlete than he. So that's how my educational enlightenment started. Slowly, with perseverance and fearlessness in the face of discriminating natives, but with a kind and patient teacher who saw artistry, humor, empathy, and brains in a slightly nervous and perceptive little boy named Isadore S. Mayputz. Thank you and R.I.P., Miss N.

7

Namely Speaking

Not only did the *loco* children of my kindergarten class look frighteningly homogenous, their names were also uncomfortably all-American sounding and easy to say. Granted, my first name WAS uncommon in these parts. And my surname was long, ungainly and seemingly difficult to properly pronounce as well, much to MY continued amazement and ire. My mostly blond and clueless classmates were called Lisa, Mary, Sylvia, Kathy, Helen, Susan, Eric, Steve, Tim, Gary, Keith, Scott, John, Mark, Kim, Dale, Nicky, etc. But at least being known as "Izzy," instead of Isadore, bailed me out among the friendlier types of townies. Mayputz, however, gave some of my classmates, and others, tongue-tying fits. I don't know why. And forget about my middle name: Schaghticoke. Wow! Well, I surmised that because the regional surnames were usually no longer than five letters in length, no one bothered to learn about, or respect, ethnic-sounding *gibberish*. It appeared to be a thing of arrogance and righteous pride among the adult villagers to purposely stumble over my family's last name as if to reinforce our *outlier* status and validate their own

25

relatedness. We were also "different and brown-skinned foreigners," and that was that. At least most of my classmates, throughout my schooling tenure with them, could accurately say my complete name with a straight face. But their small-town and small-minded parents? That's where the prejudice started and ended, thank goodness. In western N.Y., where I was born, our block had many eastern European names that I had no trouble verbalizing. Varying languages, customs, dialects, dress codes, and food were the norm as were darkish complexions and brown eyes. The adult immigrants spoke broken English at their respective jobs and in the *hood*, but continued in their native tongues at home. My first language was Estonian. Our immediate neighbors, on either side, spoke Moldovan and Polish, respectively. The friendly folks across Mills Street spoke Ukrainian. And the last names? Some were up to fourteen letters long with more consonants than necessary. And their first names? Ethnic, baby! The English spoken among our parental units was atrocious but the wide assortment of WW II "displaced persons" seemed to get everyone's names right the first time, and with much pride from all parties involved. Contrast that with the haughty, and usually intertwined, generations of *cellar dwellers* in my new town. Was it redneck laziness, false bravado, ignorance, anti-Russian sentiment, fear of communism, anger, stupidity, or overt discrimination with tinges of racism that caused "them" to garble my last name? Maybe all of the above? Was it on purpose? I don't know. And how soon "they" forgot that their own forefathers and mothers, regardless if they came over on the Mayflower or not, were also essentially immigrants at first. Anyway, I was fed up back then. I was a native-born American citizen, and still am. Do those remembrances make me upset? You bet. However, I greatly appreciated the large cadre of "enlightened" school pals, many open-minded teachers and, a few adult neighbors, that took me in as one of their own, for I was no Jones or Smith. Am I nevertheless bitter to this day for past indiscretions perpetrated on my family and me? No, not so much.

8

Sloppy Joe

We were Americans, some of us naturalized citizens, some born here. So you would think that by the time I had enrolled in kindergarten I would have tasted a good part of American cuisine, right? My mom watched the boob tube; she saw Betty Crocker commercials, Swanson TV dinners being hawked, Campbell's soup adverts, and hearty, canned Chef Boyardee products. But just to be on the safe side, I carried bagged sandwich lunches to school for the first six months of my young life. Other kids also did, but most had a hot lunch once in a while. Not me. I would bring home the weekly school menu, my mom would stare glassy-eyed at it and promptly throw it away. She repeatedly told me that I wouldn't like the food choices and would go hungry. How did she know? Just because I was a picky eater and fussed over her homemade cuisine? Perhaps HER cooking contributed to my emaciated form and lack of appetite? Heaven forbid. Maybe it was time for ME to take my taste buds for a treat? What's the worst that could happen? Well, after much wrangling on my part, she agreed to a test month. She sadly scanned the January 1965 printed lunch-meal offerings, gave me money for a yellow monthly meal ticket, and hoped for the best, as did I. It was all my idea and I hoped I would like some of the eats. At home we had soups, meats, chicken, bread, and ice cream for dessert, not exactly ethnic Estonian fare, to be sure. Those specialty foods were saved for holidays and special occasions, such as birthdays. Anyway, I thought my mouth was prepared to munch and crunch like the locals did. I was apprehensive at first but pleasantly surprised. Hot Sloppy Joe was the featured item for Monday's luncheon, along with cut green beans, cottage cheese with a pineapple slice and cherry topping, a choice of regular or chocolate milk and a cookie on the side. I had never dined on Sloppy Joe before. I got my ticket punched, put it away and sat down with my friends to sample my first school-cooked dinner. It was great. I loved the sweet tomato-infused-greasy hamburger-meat-inside-the-bun concept, ate the pineapple/cherry circle, drank the chocolate milk, and inhaled the cookie. The beans were rubbery, tasteless and off-color, and neither I nor my chums ate them or the cottage cheese. Normally I had a quirky and sensitive stomach and after dumping the remaining foodstuffs (what a waste of nutrition) into giant barrels and handing in my tray and plates to the male student dishwasher in the corner, I anxiously awaited some intestinal dysfunctions. But none came. I couldn't believe it. No grum-bellies, no flatulence, no distention, no diarrhea. Even Miss N. came over to congratulate me on my bravery and seemingly voracious hunger. That evening I excitedly told my worried mom that the food was fantastic and didn't make me ill. She seemed upset and sighed deeply. The rest of the month was filled with savory, salty and yummy dishes such as Salisbury steak, pizza, ravioli, goulash, chili, grilled cheese with green rice pudding, peas, broccoli and asparagus as the veggies. Well, the peas looked familiar, but virtually nothing else did. However, I scarfed it all down and kept it down. Then, in a bold move, I casually and gently asked my mother why SHE couldn't cook like the chintzy school cafeteria did? She got annoyed with me. She went on about having lived with Grandpa Pete's bland, no salt and no sauce diet (he mistakenly thought he had an ulcer; he just gulped his food too fast), and, my pop's desire for no-frilled, flavorless and overcooked meals. She had grown up in an authentic Estonian household filled with salt, pungent aromatic dishes, and vinegar and scallions covering the raw herring. However, she was browbeaten into cooking a "certain way" after she was first married and living with the inlaws. It seemed as though the men (my Grandpa Pete and dad) in her new immediate family had somehow become food wimps or were ahead of their time as far as healthy eating was concerned. Anyway, I kept quiet after her harried explanation as I watched her ruin a beautiful steak by searing it well done, like shoe leather, and then slathering Heinz ketchup over it because that's how my father liked it. Now I knew why I loved the school cafeteria offerings so much. Sugar, salt, spices and pepper had been missing from my diet, as well as pomegranates, artichokes and mixed fruit cups. My normally queasy mornings due to nibbling on buckwheat kasha and farina continued but now I had a delicious midday feast to look forward to. To be fair, I ate the same milk-laced breakfasts as my father did because milk was supposedly good for the digestion and ulcers. Not. My stomach curdled early and made me sick on many a morning, as happened to my dad as well. At least I got sausage and eggs for breakfast on Saturdays and Sundays, while watching Gumby and Pokey, and Davy and Goliath, on TV and I felt great.

9

Bus 57

My younger sister and I would ride this particular school bus, mostly on rainy and wintry mornings, even after we had moved into our new house and until we both respectively graduated. Our transport was small but fully functional as a traditional yellow school bus, complete with the same two interchanging bus drivers for the duration of my elementary and secondary education. B.O. was the driver as I started kindergarten. Tall, kind and enthusiastic, he was a great intermediary between my home and school. Parents trusted him with their offspring. And rightly so. He had his own children, about my age, that rode another bus in our same school system. But he was more than that. He was also a full-time farmer that milked his cows daily at 5 a.m., then drove we kids to school, then worked at the school's bus garage as a full-time mechanic, drove us home in the evening, then staggered home to milk the same bovines again. He was married, had five children, and a huge ongoing dairy operation. How he managed to get any sleep is a mystery. The guy worked hard. But why? My dad told me it was for a few bucks but primarily for the health insurance provided by the school. Lots of local farmers or their wives worked at my school, mainly for the bennies. During the course of my elementary education, sometimes B.O. was absent at the wheel. At those times M.W. would take his place. A lot older and gruffer, he was the head mechanic at the bus garage and nearing retirement. And he always wore a slimed up, gray cap, to match his workman's outfit. His wife, A., worked as the checkout lady at our cafeteria. She had that piled up hair, glasses, and gum-snapping habit going on. She was the one that punched your meal ticket full of holes around the edges. She was nice, though a bit of a stereotype. Not on purpose I hope. But whichever driver drove us, it was consistently Bus 57. It would pull up at our stop at 7:30 every morning, at the corner of Clinton and Wooley streets. Seven or eight students of different ages would be waiting there, including me. Now, I could have jumped aboard after its return trip, as some in the neighborhood did, but by then all the seats were usually taken and I didn't feel like standing. Return trip, you ask? Ha. If you climbed aboard at 7:30 a.m., you would experience a thrill ride up and down Pell Hill to pick up loads of farm kids in the rural boonies of our town. Unpaved, uneven, twisty-turny, and full of potholes, the treacherous, hilly road could have competed with a good roller coaster ride. This was the same road that had to be oiled twice yearly to keep the dust in check. The drivers had their hands full every morning constantly shifting the standard transmission and revving the engine at appropriate times to navigate that serpentine drive and not miss any corners or to literally not go off into a deep gully. However, both drivers were pros. The ride up lasted approximately 15 minutes and culminated in a top of the hill dead-end where we always had to wait for the five farm kids from the M. clan to run out to the bus. Both drivers would always wait patiently, wave to the mother, then turn the bus around slowly and zoom down the hill, picking up a few children on the way back. As I said, both drivers were experts but snow and ice can tax the best of the bunch. And one wintry day, we got stuck, and stuck good. During the snowy winter of 1965 we were coming around the corner next to Washburn's place after picking up his daughter and the bus just slid into a deep ditch. None of us wore seat belts back then because there weren't any to wear. And none of us were frightened as we slid sideways in our seats, as did the bus. B. was our surrogate father, he would know what to do. We were mired at a 45-degree angle but try as he did, he could not dislodge the bus, even though it had chains on. He kept rocking it, as our heads shot back and forth, but could not make any headway. But, just then, Old McIntyre, the farmer up the way from Washburn's, came by in his John Deere planting tractor, complete with giant clunky chains on its huge rear wheels. He had seen us go awry and quickly came to our rescue. Very nonchalantly, as he and B. briefly spoke, he put a cable around the bus's front bumper, attached the other end to the tractor's rear end and, voila: Bus 57 was pulled out onto the snowy road again. We got to school a little late and were penalized for being tardy but we had made it. I told my parents that night and they just shrugged. No big deal. Today, it would most likely be multiple cellphone 911 calls followed by the obligatory lawsuits, to boot. Back then, it was all part of life. Things happened, you know? My mother was always grateful to both drivers for taking care of her little boy, so each Christmas she would have me give them a gift. They both got the same presents: a pair of socks and smokes. B.O. got Winstons and M.W. Marlboros, which my mom had bought from the cigarette vending machine in the Grand Union grocery store. She had purchased the black woolen socks from Dewart's department store on Main Street. My pop wore the same kind of socks. The lasting memory I have of B.O.'s humanity is the time I fell asleep on the bus on the way home. It must have been a stressful day at the office for me, or maybe I had consumed too many delicious cookies with my milk that warm afternoon in Miss N.'s class. Anyway, I felt the bus turning the corner from Main Street onto Clinton Street. The next thing I remember was waking up and feeling B. carrying me to my house in his arms and my mother looking frightened and distraught. What had happened to her little Izzy that the packed bus had to park in front of my house well short of the corner? And why was I so limp looking? I regained consciousness and raced into my mother's arms. B. explained that he had seen me fall asleep while peering up into the large rear-view mirror and thought it would be nice to drop me off just this once in front of my house. But when I didn't wake up when he called my name, he stopped the bus, picked me up and literally carried me home! My mom couldn't believe it and thanked him for his consideration. They don't make men like that anymore. Thanks B.O.

10

Pee Time

It already had been a very trying day for me in the No. 1 and No. 2 departments. Firstly, in the morning, I had accidentally locked myself in the john, then with soapy and slippery hands, could not manage to twist the brass doorknob and open the door. I was momentarily panic-stricken and ended up embarrassingly knocking violently on the door to be let out. Then I had to relieve myself again, just before milk-and-cookie time commenced. What a stinky dump! It was a mess; a big waste. I emerged from the bathroom feeling lighter and hungry. However, instead of slurping down one small carton of milk with the cookies, I guzzled two, the second one courtesy of a female friend who was sweet on me. But I shouldn't have done that. At dismissal time, Miss N. routinely implored all of us to use the class bathroom one last time before our bus rides home. I never had any urgent urinary issues before so I cavalierly lined up, as always, in alphabetical order, clutched my small book bag and patiently waited. Miss N. shouted out last minute instructions for the next school day and turned the lights down low. And then I promptly pissed my pants. That darned extra pint made me do it. How awful and ignoble, standing there like a stupe, in a puddle of pee. Why hadn't I just cut out of line and sprinted to the potty if I had to go so badly? It couldn't be done, I tell you. Once the student line had formed, that was it. Conformity to adult directives and authority were paramount in those days. That's how we acted and reacted back then. I also couldn't do a "bladder dance" without attracting attention. So, I wet myself, all in the name of proper decorum and deportment. I thought I did the right thing at the time. Did I, though? Good thing the lights were dimmed because the people behind me didn't seem to notice the yellow liquid they stepped through. No one tattled or tittered in derision. I walked awkwardly and stiff-legged to my yellow school bus. Nobody took stock of my stained slacks as I carefully took a window seat and valiantly tried to shield my watery misfortune with my book bag. Luckily, no one observed my dilemma and I made sure I had on my poker face for the ride home. At my stop I bolted from the bus and ran home, into my house and quickly began to change my clothes. My suspicious mother entered my bedroom and asked me what had happened. "I had an accident," I blurted out, rather sheepishly and red-faced. She initially linked the word accident to some sort of bloodletting but then realized what had really transpired. She laughed when I angrily blamed that extra milk I had drunk. And I'm sure Miss N. and Mr. "Monster," the elementary school custodian, had at least a chuckle upon seeing that yellow spill on the white linoleum of the classroom floor. However, as the year continued, I became vigilant and paranoid as to my bladder capacity and had no more "accidents." Other kids, not so much. I also stepped through various disgusting discharges while in that dismissal line. I surmised that other kids had periodic "incontinence" issues as well. But no one said a word. We all got through pee time, which was not nearly as gross as vomit time, which was usually a daily spontaneous occurrence. At least it was in my class. I'm sure things are similar in today's elementary schools. I don't envy modern kindergarten teachers trying to teach self-entitled and narcissistic little tykes anything, especially since most don't yet have a firm grasp on their mental or bodily functions. They are most probably too busy clutching their cellphones while defecating anywhere and everywhere. Oh, brave new world.

11

Fire Drilling

My first fire drill was downright scary. However, we were casually warned about them by our teacher. Nevertheless, when the strange, loud, pinging bell went off unexpectedly that morning, we kindergartners froze in our seats and stared wide-eyed at Miss N. for guidance. She would know what to do, and she did. As the clanging sound continued to echo in our room, she quickly lined us up and had us briskly follow her to the nearest exit door and out onto the playground. No one lagged, no one dawdled, no one talked as we gathered around her like goslings surrounding a mother goose. But I don't remember if Miss N. had checked our class bathroom or "cot room" to see if any students got left behind. I suppose she did when I wasn't paying attention. She led the way out and we young'uns followed obediently. Woe to those who did not. After the whole school disgorged its load of "scholars," it was time to go back inside again. Luckily, the weather had been cooperative because we had run out without hats and coats on. The other students all around us slowly and silently filed back into their respective classrooms, heads hung low, with slumped shoulders and downcast eyes. Hey, a five-minute break was still a break! Now, back to treading water again. By the way, during my grammar school career, we had many fire drills but never a real fire, not even our town's lone fire truck ever showed up. Oh, well.

12

Morning Blather

You had to be in your seat, with hands clasped together on top of your desk, and ready to listen. Listen to the teacher? Listen to your boisterous compatriots trying to settle down? No, it was 8:30 a.m., so Miss N. said, and time for morning announcements over the class loudspeaker. Those gruff, five-minute speeches by Principal H. set the tone for the day. In his gravelly baritone voice, as if he had just extinguished a cigarette and polished off a tumbler full of bourbon, he would slowly and deliberately outline any significant recent past events, student accomplishments, and to proceed to spew out the current day's agenda. It was another daily ritual for we beginners. Our kindergarten days were filled with lessons on deportment and other socially acceptable behaviors, on top of the learnin' we were gettin'. Children that were easily molded, or at least played along with the gag, thrived. Those that railed against the "machine," or were born incorrigible, had it rough. Some were held back, some repeatedly disciplined, some were asked not to return. Kindergarten seemed a happy and safe place to play and learn but you had to toe the line early and hear out that morning jibber-jabber from the principal.

13

The Flunkees

The attrition of my fellow mates, both female and male, started early, with no regard to feelings or future mental trauma. If you could not spell your name or tie your shoes, forgot to use toilet paper after a dump, or know what day it was, you were held back, period. You would be repeating kindergarten, or first grade, or any elementary grade as deemed necessary by the *teacher's committee*. It was a cruel twist of fate for some students. Since we had no nursery schools or pre-K in our dink-hole village, all appropriately aged youngsters were welcome to start kindergarten. Some were obviously not ready for the rigors of prime time. Others, like myself, were more than prepared and ready for the challenges ahead, like lunch, naptime, recess, milk and cookie time, and playtime. When did we learn anything? Anyway, some classmates just couldn't cut it. Maybe it was naptime that flummoxed and flunked a few of them? What a bullshit travesty of justice. At the end of the school year Miss N. gently told our class who was going to be held back and to be extra nice to those students should we run into them next year. Of course they were ridiculed and ostracized by us immediately and ceased being our friends. They were the dummies, we the smart ones that had made it to first grade! However, the fear of failure instilled in the rest of us was palpable, regardless of our knowing sighs and blustery self-absorbed clamor. I'm sure the flunked out students' pain continued unabated because they had the stigma of being losers and were now considered as *second class* the rest of the elementary school way-socially, psychologically and scholastically. Sure, we had Special Ed back then and BOCES, but those programs were reserved for specially designated children, not the flunkees. And we didn't have an elementary school psychologist to help soften the blow either. In today's world of political correctness and esteem building at all cost, I wonder if ANY of those failed students would have been left behind. In my day, it was evolutionary; the best and the brightest proceeded while the "dumbbells" were forgotten about. Today it would be considered revolutionary and reactionary. I admit to being a teaser of the fallen lot at times although I also admit to being one of the few students that still sporadically and heretically talked and played with the failed few. I'm sure the rejected and dejected appreciated it, too. Maybe. What a way to start life: winners and losers from the get-go. And no whining allowed.

14

Dressing the Part

The clothes make the man or so "they" say. Well, oftentimes I would take the Halloween concept to extremes when I played *make believe*, either alone or with close, like-minded fellows. For me it wasn't good enough to pretend to be a "cowboy;" I had to have the full regalia: hat, vest, boots, holsters and toy revolver six-shooters. It was important to look the part and not just play it. My boyhood pals weren't as persnickety and used their index fingers for shootin' irons. Such peasants. Granted that most of my superhero and "play" costumes were not store bought, nevertheless, they functioned to bolster my fertile and detailed imagination. My mom indulged my playful fantasies and expertly cobbled/sewed together outfits for me. Nothing complicated or elaborate: a cape here, a hat there.... But I always appreciated her efforts, nonetheless. My dress-up phase eventually faded as elementary school progressed. Although as I matured and willingly participated in numerous high school theatrical productions, as well as musicals and orchestral recitals, there appeared ample opportunities for me to *dress the part*. Watching my own young offspring catch the acting bug, and revel in wearing outlandish outfits while playing, brought back memories and certain melancholy feelings of my artistic expressions of yesteryear. Their many props and outfits packed a few large trunks and not just dresser drawers in our home. Was it something in the family genes that made them act so? The need to wear "appropriate" attire as needed? And did that feeling ever really completely recede? Maybe not. I had to dress in a uniform, as a former pharmacist, and currently wear an office-mandated scrubs outfit, as a dentist. Anyhow, perhaps a lifetime spent in "proper garb" has made me loathe clothes shopping and clothing in general. Maybe it's a heterosexual male thing or, most likely, it is me. Luckily, hottie blondie, my beautiful and usually amazingly kitted-out wife, knows my various bodily sizes and shops for me, whenever SHE deems necessary. Only in half jest do I proclaim to be a part-time naturist. My wife insists that I still look sexy without coverings on my bod. As a *dirty* old coot, I'll take that compliment any time.

15

Rip Van Freddie

Poor Freddie loved to sleep, and sleep some more. Naptime in kindergarten turned into a bedtime ritual for him, complete with pajamas and his own personal pillow and blankie. Mandatory napping in our all-day class started immediately after lunch. Of course, a belly full of warm food sometimes induced somnolence but Freddie took it to the next level. We would walk back into our room after chowing down in the cafeteria and Miss N. would quickly select two "volunteers" to distribute the folded blue cots from the "cot room" at the back of the class. She then dimmed the overhead lights and closed the clangy metal window blinds as each student flopped down onto her/his cot on the floor. Having a somewhat nervous disposition, I would curl up in a ball and stare into space for the half hour lie-down. I never felt drowsy during naptime. After a few minutes into every daily nap, I would hear that telltale snoring sound and chuckle to myself. It was Freddie, who else? Everyone heard it but no one said a word. Not a peep was allowed by our teacher. I could not tell time yet but knew that when the big hand on the large wall clock pointed straight down Miss N. would abruptly draw the blinds and light up the room. I would usually bolt upright and start folding up my cot. Most students were groggy and awakened slowly, but they arose nonetheless. Not Freddie; he was still sawing wood amid our noise and chatter. Sometimes some of we wiseacres would gather around his "bed" and stare in amazement. He would have his shoes and socks removed and stacked neatly at the foot of the cot, along with his pile of clothing. His blanket was pulled up to his chin. The lights were on, the afternoon sun was blazing through the glass panes as kindly Miss N. would implore us, in a whisper, to leave him alone. She would crack a benevolent smile as we laughed softly. Finally, he stirred. He always looked sheepish and out-of-sorts upon joining the living. But by the time he had gotten dressed and put away his cot, the rest of the class had already learned something new. And by the time he was fully functional, it was storytime, then milk-and-cookie time, and then dismissal. His pattern of behavior persisted all the school year. Well, Freddie didn't make it out of kindergarten. His slumberous ways had gotten the best of him. He was held back. I still don't know why the lovely and genial Miss N. didn't force him to do more, to stay awake, to keep him roused, or something. It's as if she just knew that he wasn't ready to move on with the rest of the herd and needed that extra shuteye. His soporific ways most likely cost him friends and even hurt his psyche. Perhaps? I do know that I never associated with him again, even on the playground. Failure is a bitch. That's life, though. I hope Freddie started drinking industrial strength coffee at some point in his life.

Take a break!

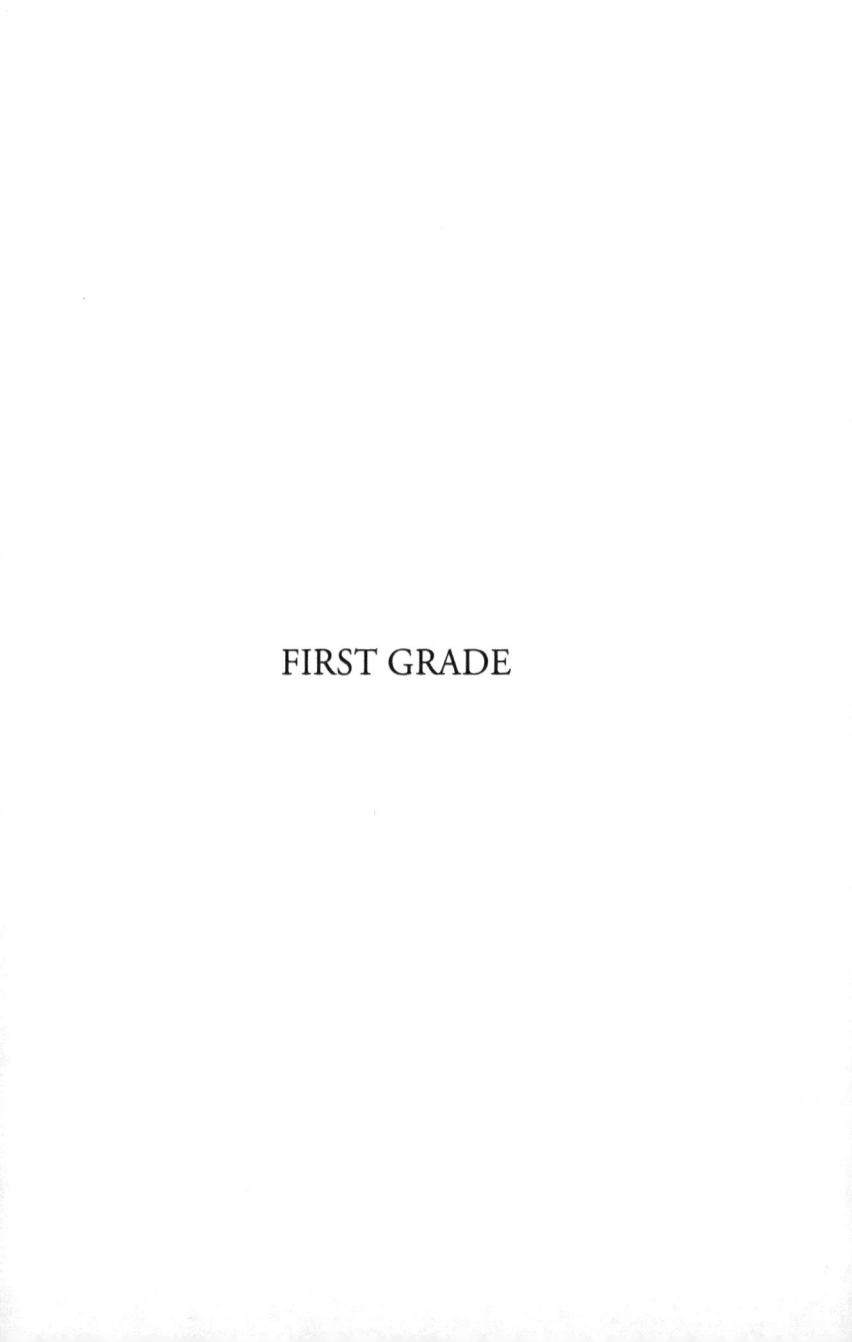

FIRST GRADE

16

Furgie

Furgie and her family lived in a small house, on a steep incline, perched at the top of Wooley Street and kitty-corner to my bus stop. However, as a corollary to Murphy's Law, Furgie and her younger siblings were ALWAYS late for the bus, even though they resided no more than fifty feet from the stop! That was strike number one. Strike number two was that neither she, her brother or sister ever offered an apology for their lateness. No contrition, not even something mumbled. Nothing. It didn't seem to matter that we were waiting for them on most mornings, getting aggravated in the process, and hoping we got to school on time. B.O., the usual bus driver, just shook his head as they eventually piled in and took their seats. Strike three came when Furgie contentedly stuck the index finger of her right hand into her mouth and started sucking it. No kidding. And this would transpire nearly every morning. Three strikes and Furgie was out. That's when the vehement teasing began. And not just from me, but from virtually all the young men on the bus. She would try and hide her habit by scrunching down in her seat or by ducking behind her brother's misshaped and shaved head. Sometimes she even sassed us back. Granted, if she had been attractive and svelte, we probably would have left her alone. Maybe. However, she wasn't. Chubby, with a homemade, bowl haircut and a spittle-laced, bodacious disposition, she became a prime target of our infantile derision. It was just too easy. The bus driver tried to intervene on many occasions during our spontaneous outbursts of wordy misbehavior, but failed to quell us. No one swore but the hate-filled diatribes were usually tearfully hurtful to her, nonetheless. Interestingly, her addled brother and dorky sister were never the brunt of our assault, only she. The really funny part was that once we arrived at school, all teasing had ceased. Although she was in many of my classes early on, I never lobbed any derogatory words her way during school hours or even when on the playground. It was a bus ride *schtick* only. My bus buddies and I verbally tortured her for years, until she moved out of our area after sixth grade. We had lost our easy mark, darn it. Looking back, we were definitely bullies, myself included. We acted shamefully and in a misogynistic way against a defenseless girl. I still feel very embarrassed all these years later. Furgie, I'm sorry. My heartfelt apologies to you. Nevertheless, I wonder if you ever ballooned up to be as large as your obnoxious mother was?

17

The New Math

I didn't know it at the time but every few years my elementary education would convulse with a "new math" directive that would confuse the students, parents and teachers. It was ALL new to me at first; I was only in first grade at the time of the initial onslaught of that poorly thought out decree. I recall bringing home my textbooks for my father to put brown paper bag protective covers on and his remarking about my math book. It said *Today's New Arithmetic* on the front cover. He dutifully copied that title onto the book cover he had just made, then pondered aloud what was so new about arithmetic. As a civil engineering college professor, his kind of figuring and calculating began with algebra, culminating with calculus and differential equations. He briefly leafed through my book and laughed out loud in disdain. "Why do 'they' insist on changing math every year?," he remarked. "It hasn't changed since Pythagoras' time in ancient Greece," he further quipped. I guess he knew about the space age we were now in and how all Americans and their offspring had to keep up with the "new" times. His own college students must have told him that they too had "new math" in their previous respective high schools. Anyhow, it was all confusing to me, new or not. I was now in first-grade with that dreaded Mrs. H. She was a no-nonsense, middle-aged woman with ugly looking glasses and a screechy voice. It was a bad start to the school year. Kindergarten had been a blast, first grade would be a bear. Naptime was reduced to putting your head on your desk for twenty minutes with the lights off. You got only one cookie at milk-and-cookie time. And you had to raise your hand to go to the lavatory and be acknowledged before you could relieve yourself. And on top of all that, scary Mrs. H., with those black, horn-rimmed glasses that looked as though horns were coming out of her head, made things even more difficult because of her meanness and mannerisms. What saved my sanity was reading, printing and an early sense of levity. I could read quickly and print letters and words better than anyone in my class, and received plenty of gold stars for my efforts. Must have been genetics. However, my father, also a gifted artist and calligrapher, was never duly impressed with my printing awards and sarcastically called my labors chicken scratches with a lead pencil. Boy, was he tough. Oh, well. Science and social studies were solid for me, too. The mathematics portion managed to kill me, however. I started flunking arithmetic early in the year and Mrs. H. was of no help to me. Other students were also doing badly and her tyrannical outbursts of frustration at our idiocy only compounded our failure to understand her. Yes, I comprehended the basic tenets; I could add and subtract. However, sets, subsets, prime numbers, wtf? I needed help and so I asked my mom. She in turn asked my pop. Big mistake. When he found out I was flailing in math, he went on the warpath, admonishing me for being so stupid. How could HIS son not understand the logic, simplicity and beauty of numbers? Was I really genetically related to him or not? I cried while doing my homework. It just wasn't sinking in. My father's passive-aggressive belittling of me wasn't helping matters, either. So, HE went to see Mrs. H., but I wasn't present during his meeting with her. I heard it turned into somewhat of a shouting match with Mrs. H. finally stepping off. At first my father's thick accent caused her to think he was an uncouth ignoramus until he angrily informed her of his status as a professor at the college in town. Then he went up and down her by yelling about the "new math" nonsense that I had to learn. It didn't end well as he was asked to leave the elementary school by the principal. At home, my usually mild-mannered father was mad at me, Mrs. H., and the whole darn school system. However, first grade numerology gradually started to make more sense to me. Maybe it was because Mrs. H. started teaching it better. Maybe SHE finally understood it better? Things cooled off at home as my GPA improved. My old man just shook his head and told me to anticipate more of the same in future grades. I will tell you that math, new or not, was never a favorite subject of mine. And the first math that I understood well was algebra, but that was in ninth grade, a lifetime of agony away. Meanwhile, the numbers game kept shifting in elementary school, all the way to sixth grade, with my dad smirking and insulting me the whole way. Mrs. H. had done the best she could and maybe my father's tirade made her realize that she was also guilty of not knowing the material. I passed first grade and still hated numbers. But a curious thing occurred many years later between Mrs. H. and my parents. Not only did they become friends but Mrs. H. and her husband became somewhat more prosperous and began selling prime, butchered meats from their farm to people in town, including my folks. I found out about those monkeyshines as a college student and reminded my mother about what a piece of work Mrs. H. had been. "Ancient history," said my dad. My mom agreed and said she was a nice, old retired teacher that now sold "organic" sides of beef and pork. End of story. Really? How could they take her side? How could my father let her get away with it? Was I the only numbskull that couldn't learn *simple* arithmetic back then? Was Mrs. H. vindicated in the end? She had made my young life miserable in her classroom. But some kids GOT the mathematical concepts without intervening parental units; just not me. I guess I was the dummy after all. I'll have to live with that notion, darn it.

18

Show and Tell

Personalities and character were blatantly bared whenever it was time for early morning Show and Tell. Those children who were born confident strode to the front of the class and seemed unembarrassed to show us something or to describe some event in their mostly uninteresting lives. Others, easily coerced by Mrs. H., did not enjoy the brief limelight and stuttered and stammered through the ordeal, sometimes quickly running back to their seats all red-faced when finished. I was more of an introvert, and still am; an observant outsider looking in. Not one to boldly lead and divulge secrets, but one to cleverly suggest provocative solutions for pressing situations; and sometimes, to reply with a snarky, levitous tongue. Most of the same brave kids repeatedly hogged the spotlight and I was content with that paradigm, respectfully watching and listening to them. Mrs. H. valiantly tried to hornswoggle me up there but to no avail. However, one day I brought in a black swallowtail caterpillar, housed in a small glass jar, with parsley, and a stick inside. I nodded to Mrs. H. that I was ready to talk, and she knowingly nodded back to me. She officially "introduced" me to my bewildered classmates.

What was HE doing up there? They thought I was sort of shy. Funny yes, but shy nonetheless. Finally, I had a chance to open my pie-hole and vocalize about something near and dear to me. I got so engrossed about butterfly life cycles, metamorphosis, skin shedding of caterpillars and frass, that I forgot about the time limit, but no one seemed to care. Even my closest friends were shocked at my entomological knowledge. I didn't sweat, didn't trip over words and delivered a decent talk about a relatively common butterfly larvae, found in most area gardens. But I never "showed and told" again. I didn't have to. I left that up to the same hotshots as before, those who always had something to say, regardless of how mundane or inane their topics usually were. I had my new street cred and effectively *retired*. Mrs. H. never bugged me again.

19

Meats and Mead

After the butcher on Main Street finally shuttered his doors in the mid-sixties, where was my mom going to buy fresh meats from? According to her, the Victory and Grand Union supermarkets had steaks that looked like someone had wiped their bottoms on them. Definitely not appetizing. And driving to the nearby city for a slice of sirloin was a waste of time and gas. Enter Fokay's Market. Although on my mom's food gathering trail, she seldom frequented that long established but hole-in-the-wall emporium, housed in two adjoining original buildings on Main Street. However, many discerning villagers did. Owned by a large local family descended from old Russian immigrants who came over to America prior to 1900, they were fully interbred, through various marriages, into the scuzzy fabric of the area. But they keenly understood my parent's relatively newbie immigrant status and one day personally invited my mom for a tour of their recently revamped store and newly opened liquor establishment. It had been a smart business move. Their expanded butcher section in the rear of the store, run by old Mr. Fokay's slightly younger brother, harkened back to the butcher shops of Europe, and now also sold fish. My mom was in heaven and duly impressed. Even though she was already acquainted with the store, she had rarely bought anything there besides cold cuts such as bologna and tavern loaf. Also, all the prices were one to three cents higher than on the same foodstuffs found across the street at the Grand Union. Sometimes we would catch old Mrs. Fokay herself, running between stores, comparing and setting her store fees based on the supermarket's expenses. However, the enlarged poultry, beef, pork, seafood, and deli departments were now truly inviting. And, with a fully stocked wine and spirit store next door, Fokay's became the "new" place to shop, at least for protein purchases and booze. Buying a bottle of red wine, some thick pork chops and a whole herring wrapped in newspaper began a weekly tradition for our family, with minor alterations in the meats chosen. I usually accompanied my mom and baby sister on Saturday shopping trips and took in all the scents and sights of those hokey and old-fashioned food and libation marts. Fokay's Market lasted for decades, long after the two large and *modern* chain markets in town had gone belly-up. Friendly "family" service, great choices and cuts of meats, and a mead station, as well. What was not to like?

20

Sour Notes

Once a week Miss R., the elementary school music teacher, would visit our class and try to educate we cretins in the fundamentals of music. I had already begun official but rudimentary piano lessons and greatly enjoyed the weekly meetings with her. She was a rather large, bosomy woman, compared to Mrs. H., my wisp of a first grade teacher. Miss R. always entered our classroom with a tumultuous swoosh and quickly started to enunciate loudly and succinctly. We students scrambled to keep up after putting away our textbooks and papers. Those that had an inkling about middle C, 4/4 time, treble clef, etc., usually fared well, others, not really. Her humungous and tattered shopping bag often contained tambourines, triangles, xylophones, and recorders as props. She would also draw chalkboard notes and babble on about musical theory. It was all too much for most students. SHE was too much, too enthusiastic, if you know what I mean. Then she would play some of those funky transportable instruments from her old bag. It was sometimes hilarious as she spoke, played, and tried to teach us an hour's worth of music in a half-hour's allotted time. She got lathered up, while many of my pals just sat there stone cold, confused and dopey looking. Anyhow, once in a while, she would pass out green colored plastic recorders to we dummies, you know, those instruments with holes down the front side, vaguely resembling oboes or clarinets. You exhaled forcefully in one end and covered up the holes with your fingers, at intervals, to make sounds. Miss R. would direct us to play simple tunes while stomping her huge feet to keep the correct beat going. It was a cacophony of horrible sounding bedlam. She persevered on her own recorder while we dutifully blew our brains out. It was terrible but entertaining. And I never found out how she sterilized the mouth parts of those "green flutes" when going from class to class. I guess I never asked. The rest of the year, as well as for the tenure of elementary school, she kept showing up like an unwanted gypsy carpetbagger. She was one stubborn lady and never gave up. At least I appreciated her and probably learned something along the way when I wasn't laughing.

21

Primitive HIPAA

HIPAA stands for Health Insurance Portability and Accountability Act and serves to protect patients' privacy rights but has also, rather sarcastically and ubiquitously, become synonymous with all "secretive" issues in today's world. Was our elementary school way ahead of its time by invoking "privacy laws" when our marks were disbursed to us every quarter? At the end of that fateful Friday afternoon, Mrs. H. solemnly and slowly walked down our rows and, with the slightest hint of ritualistic swagger, handed out our quarterly transcript reports. However, we were repeatedly warned NOT to discuss or show our grades to anyone, not even our best friends. Only our moms and dads had the privilege to review them. Allowed to glance briefly at them, we then had to quickly stow away those A, B, and C-laden, stiff, yellow-colored pieces of doom/delight in our book bags and prepare for dismissal. Those were the days, before the new-fangled grading system emerged and came into vogue, using I's, N's and P's in hopes of psychologically snookering angry parents. In our day, an A was an A, an F was an F, and everyone knew what they meant. We left the school building to board our respective buses, and that's where HIPAA hit its weak link and was thrown out the window. Kids instantly whipped out their report cards and nonchalantly compared them, especially if they were buddies. As the bus ride continued, sometimes there would be wholesale trading of the cards, to get a better look. Children can be nosy, after all. Obviously, the bus drivers were IN on the "privacy policy" but did virtually nothing to quash the curious minded minions. One time a major skirmish was narrowly averted by M.W., our gruff, elderly and sometime bus driver. It turned out that someone had purposely and roughly snatched the report card of a certain unpopular girl and passed it around the back of the bus, to much ridicule and laughter. Well, the girl wailed in protest and wouldn't stop her shrill shrieking. M.W. finally pulled the bus over in a screeching halt, got up off his seat and menacingly made his way to the rear of Bus 57, which took about five steps, mind you. He knew who started the fracas and physically plopped him back into his seat, wrested the mangled and tattered report card away from a melee participant, and returned it to Furgie – the distressed girl. No one messed with old M.W. He yelled and admonished the guilty for exhibiting such poor and stupid behavior. I just sat there, near the front, innocently, but had nonetheless heard and seen all the commotion. He restarted the bus and we continued. The back row parties were now sullen and quiet, Furgie noisily sucked her index finger, and M.W. made his scheduled stops. All back to normal. Of course the incident became the buzz of my classroom the next Monday because Furgie was in my class. Chagrined Mrs. H. rolled her eyes in disdain and frustration; she didn't know what to say. The "bus fight," the mad bus driver, the torn report card, Furgie's finger, etc. It was tough to enforce HIPAA-type rules back then, and it still is.

22

Assemblies

Goody, a chance to get away from a usually unpleasant Mrs. H. and my anxiety-laden first grade classroom. Assemblies: Those gatherings of young people in the assembly hall which also doubled as our gymnasium, in planned outings to further educate we neophytes in various school approved subjects. Sometimes it was a magic show, other times a scientific discourse on plants. And sometimes just a serious and dogmatic freewheeling and rambling diatribe by Principal H., on staying drug and alcohol free. What? I was only in first grade. Give me a break. Bong hits and *free love* would come much, much later for me. Woodstock hadn't even happened, yet! And there we were, listening to the dangers of addiction and, worse, sexual attraction between the sexes! Wow. But it still was a break from the boring droning of my teacher and I was always grateful. Somehow the assemblies were never announced but sprung on us as a benevolent treat. And they were, for the most part. First grade sucked for me; any distraction was greatly appreciated. Assemblies, lunchtime, recess, naptime on my desk top, etc., were treasured respites from that exasperated and perplexed Mrs. H. Second grade had to be better, and it was.

23

Raw Carrots and Cheese

I ate my cookie, guzzled down my milk and prepared to go home. Those were the last activities of the class day right before dismissal. I had sugar floating in my tummy upon arriving home but was still famished after a hard day in first grade. Out came my "home" snacks or, should I say, homely snacks? Carefully doled out by my mother, those after school treats were not Twinkies or Drake's Cakes. No, I was handed a large, peeled, raw carrot stick and one square of frozen Kraft American sliced cheese. And no seconds, lest I spoiled my appetite for dinner, later in the evening. I crunched the bland offerings daily without complaining and then usually scurried outside to play, weather permitting. Months later, as an invitee to an after-school playdate, I would sample my first savory Hostess Ho Ho. Sublime and decadent is how it tasted. I never told my Mom. I'm sure she knew what indulgences other housewives were serving their progeny but her own son got carrots and hard cheese. Was she merely frugal or nutritionally ahead of her time? Maybe both?

24

Monkey Bars

Of course we had vigilant, glaucoma-addled, old ladies as playground monitors. And they did watch us and holler out if there was imminent risk to we rascals. Roughhousing, fighting, wrestling, and even teasing were definitely not allowed. But what about the hazards of the playground apparatus strewn about haphazardly at the back of the elementary school lawn? We were not oblivious to the possible dangers of the welded iron monkey bar set-up, which sat upon hard packed dirt, or the metal chained swing sets with either deadly wooden seats or ass pinching and uncomfortable rubber straps, and the rusted metal seesaws, as well as the four, all metal, spring loaded riding horses. We played fearlessly, yet somehow warily knew not only our physical limitations but the inherent risks associated with the equipment that was there for our recreation. Were we tough or just plain stupid? Did we unknowingly take more personal responsibility for our actions back then? We saw and felt the hard iron bars, the bone hard ground underneath those bars, the unyielding wooden swing set seats, etc. There was no margin for error. We had to be careful when playing.

Personal responsibility, baby! There were no helicopter parents hovering over or even near us. Perhaps our relatively cautious natures did not make monkeys of us, after all. Few, if any of my friends and fellow classmates ever busted anything or lost any teeth. We all got our obligatory bumps and bruises and that's all. There was never a bloody line of students at the nurse's office after recess periods. Somehow we managed not to mangle our bodies amid all the steel set out for us. Obviously, safety standards have evolved, as they should have. But with the advent of outdoor soft plastic jungle gyms, rubber slides, automobiles that practically drive themselves, and smartphones that make decisions for us, we have become mollycoddled wimps in all walks of life and have effectively abrogated our mental and physical prowesses to machines and other humans. And, as soon as "one more thing goes wrong," it seems that our nation of massively stressed out but "entitled" people, on their last nerves, lash out, and sometimes wreak havoc on innocents because they cannot fathom losing, ridicule or criticism. "Society" has let them down, suddenly damaged their already fragile egos and self-esteems and "needs to pay." Is our present social structure, especially in schools, based on blaming others for our own shortcomings? I think so, but I'm not a psychiatrist, psychologist or sociologist and have no expertise in those areas. Just common sense.   Landing hard on your noggin after falling off the monkey bars, because you were a klutz, was your own fault in 1966. In 2018, it is everyone else's fault, and you weren't even hurt because of the rubberized padding you fell onto. How times have changed.

25

The Great Sickness

It was most probably influenza but my parents didn't know for sure. I was really sick as a dog: headaches, high fever, sore throat, and feeling woozy and tired. It could have just been a very bad cold, however. Obviously, I was kept home from school, but one day morphed into five. It was torture to remain basically bedridden and feeling lousy for a whole school week. That just added to my stress. I knew that Mrs. H. wouldn't care and expect me to not only make up the missed school work but be up on the latest knowledge. She had no outward empathy or sympathy for the weak and meek. Maybe she was hardened this way by her hardscrabble life, married to a poor farmer living outside our village. Whatever the reason, she was a tough-ass bitch as a first grade teacher. I didn't like her when I was feeling well. Now I would be in real trouble when I got back. However, I needed to get healthy first. Enter OUR town physician, Dr. K. "Kleppie," as my old man called him, was a short-statured, elderly, general medical practitioner originally from Switzerland who had his home office in the center of town. Patient hours were from 5 to 8 p.m. Monday through Friday only. He visited his hospital patients in the mornings and made *house calls* the rest of the day. That's right, house calls, complete with his black leather bag and old-fashioned stethoscope. He was a widower with a son in medical school and an older daughter married to an attorney, living in a nearby municipality. He had lots of time on his hands. His staff at his house practice consisted of only himself. Although there were two other doctors in the area and a few at the local hospital, many patients preferred him to the others. Maybe it was his knowledgeable sounding European accent, or his smart and spotless, white Ford Mercury, or his widower status. Whatever, he was OUR family physician and my parents stuck with him. My dad instructed he and his son in tennis for free during the summer months, so our family always got to see him in a timely manner. There was no queue for us. One hand washes the other, you know. When he received the call that I was badly ailing, he immediately arrived at our doorstep. I could hear his car brakes squeal as he stopped on a dime in front of our rented home. The beloved and respected Dr. K. was in the house! He gingerly walked into my bedroom, sat on the edge of the bed and started to examine me. I wasn't nervous, I knew him well from past office encounters. He didn't wear a mask, gloves or wash his hands; he didn't need to, he was a doctor. Plus it was

1966. Germs were stupid back then, remember? He listened to my heart, took my pulse and temperature, patted me on the head, conferred with my parents, and promptly left, but not before collecting five bucks from my old man and issuing his standard mantra: Plenty of sleep, plenty of sunshine, aspirin for fever, and applesauce for diarrhea. Strangely, I started to feel better right after he departed. He was a magician, that man. Well, I started to improve that whole weekend but dreaded going back to school and facing Mrs. H. again. I really hated her, that witch. I appeared first at the school nurse's station the following Monday to get logged back in and give her my excuse. Missing a week of school was a big deal back then. I slowly walked to my classroom and was instantly surrounded by my buddies who welcomed me back. It was a good feeling. But then Mrs. H. broke up our little ad hoc party, my frightened pals hightailed it back to their seats, and she just stood over me and glared. Then the funniest thing happened. She asked me how I felt and said that she missed having me in her class. She missed my sense of humor and my gold-star-worthy printing. Then she *smiled*. I backed up to my desk and chair and plopped down, while keeping her in sight. NO word was spoken of my missed assignments. Was this some sort of a set up? I was highly suspicious, as always, but needn't have been.

She had finally bared her emotions for me; I was puzzled but elated. Maybe she wasn't that bad after all? Perhaps beneath that prickly exterior was a first grade teacher that cared, regardless of her alleged domestic turmoil? Perhaps.

26

Back for a Visit

My family and I were fully invested in our new country digs but my widowed and recently retired paternal grandfather was still holding down the old homestead in the city from whence we came. I heard he was lonely, with no kingdom to rule; basically no one to boss around anymore. Plus there was the scuttlebutt in our household that he planned on selling his house and move in with us. My mom was horrified at that prospect. Nevertheless, it seemed to be inevitable. In the meantime we visited him as often as possible, on most major holidays and for extended periods during the summers after my kindergarten and first grade years. As a professor, my pop had summers off, so off we scooted to see the self-appointed patronizing patriarch! I vividly recall running out of the elementary school on the last day of first grade, waving both arms, clutching my initialed and worn canvas book bag, my report card, and flying into my dad's car that was running and waiting for me in front of the school. There were no goodbyes to the teacher or friends, I just wanted to get the hell out of Dodge. First grade had been a major hassle and unkind to my ego and scholastic potential. Mrs. H. had thwarted me at every step it seemed, and I was so done with that bitchy farmer's wife. Our family station wagon was a welcome sight as I literally jumped inside it. I had received all A's on my transcript and was relieved, not proud, just relieved. I didn't want to hear any guff from my pop, not after the year I had. An added inducement for my excellent scholarship was our planned excursion to Crystal Beach Amusement Park, just over the border in Canada, relatively close to Niagara Falls. Having gotten straight A's on my report card garnered me free admission to the park and rides. Bonus! I could already taste the chocolate ice cream cones as we began our drive into the slowly setting sun. Riding in an automobile was a *trip* for me in those days. My baby sister sat on my mom's lap, I stood on the center console with my head propped up against the roof of the car, and my pop drove one-handed. No one was buckled up. How irresponsible and naïve we were back then. Of course, only two lap belts were standard in the front seats anyway. The westward day trip had us stop first at my mom's parents' home, which was on the way. They were city dwellers, too. And they were also Estonian immigrants still working at maintaining their American Dream. They had their own house, cars, etc., and did well for themselves, although a strictly frugal lifestyle overshadowed their niggardly incomes. It was the same in my family. But that's how most immigrants got ahead in America. They worked hard and didn't spend foolishly. No movies, no dining out, no nothing. Gee, I think I learned something from my folks, after all! Anyway, my maternal grandparents were heavily involved in their church and always had some kind of an Orthodox function to attend, especially my grandfather. He was the big cheese and head of his church board, etc. He personally hired and fired priests like George Steinbrenner used to do with his beleaguered manager, Billy Martin. I never realized that "winning" and power were such important religious doctrines. I guess God also appreciated a winner, at least in my grandpa's mind. So, we visited, ate traditional Estonian vittles and fixings for dinner, stayed overnight and then proceeded to drive to the next big city and crashed in our old aqua-green colored house. We had made it. My former Mills Street friends showed up after a few days when they got word that I was back in the *hood*. It was nice to see them again, but I had changed. We talked, watched Batman on TV together, played "army" in my old backyard, ran around as superheroes in capes and ate at one another's homes. However, I was different now. I felt differently. My country town was wide open, my new backyard was large, my new street was gigantic. Even my new friends were big.

Getting used to my former small house, yard, and scrawny and tawdry fellas took a while. I wanted to go back to the wilderness, again. I didn't belong here anymore. My Polish boyhood friend Steve W. came over, played with my toys instead of me, just like old times, and ate my leftover food during lunch. Nothing had changed and maybe that was the problem. I had grown intellectually, but my *city peeps* seemed to have not. Although in a large metropolis, they appeared stultified by their immediate surroundings and parochial existence, ensconced in a tribal-like state, in the "safety" of their block and limited community of similar ethnic consorts. I had the freedom to explore my village, unencumbered by property lines, fences or crime. They did not have that advantage or privilege. I was blessed and happy that we had moved out of that rattrap of a city. We stayed for a month and then drove back east to our "country" rental apartment. It was a grueling six-hour bumpy ride, on hilly and scenic back roads with lots of potholes. And my immediate family's prediction slowly came true. My Grandpa Pete had put his house on the market for sale and was poised to join us, much to my mom's dismay.

Take a break!

SECOND GRADE

27

Mr. "Monster"

Our second-grade classroom was suddenly overrun by stink bugs that sunny and warm autumn morning. Kindly Mrs. Hutch…. did not like anything buggy, and those nickel-sized, green and brown insects made her visibly squeamish. I, on the other hand, petted them gently as they walked against the windows of our room (they turn malodorous if roughly handled or squeezed). I loved all things slithery or with wings, and those pesky bugs (they are true bugs) were a familiar and welcome sight to me. Well, Mrs. Hutch…. had had enough. She motioned to me and whispered to go find Mr. "Monster," the school custodian and to beckon him to rush over and deal with our "little problems," as she succinctly put it. I stared questioningly at her and she added that she trusted me to find him quickly and not wander the halls or get into trouble. Our families knew one another. Her husband and my pop both taught in the same department at our town's college. Plus I had a rising reputation of coming through during crunch time. You could always depend on little Izzy to finish what he started, be it athletically or scholastically. I knew where Mr. "Monster's" office was and did not relish the prospect of walking in there alone. As kindergarteners we were all introduced to him at an assembly and he became part of the crew that would "educate" us. We heard his name mentioned and cringed in fear. He was very tall, barrel-chested, bald, and with big ears that stuck out. He had a huge, toothy cake-hole and large, calloused hands. We were told he was a full-time farmer that worked in our school during the days. It was his sole job to clean our rooms, fix things and help the teachers and principal keep order in the place. He was scary, nonetheless. I knocked softly on his office door and just stood there motionless, hoping he had heard. The door creaked open and he peered down at me like Frankenstein's creation would have. I cleared my throat and timidly said, "Mr. Monster, Mrs. Hutch…. sent me to get you for our room." He laughed in halting guffaws. I didn't get it. Then in a booming voice he retorted, "My name is Mr. M…., not Mr. Monster." I was confused. His last name sounded like monster when spoken rapidly. He was a gargantuan human in size, as well. It all seemed to fit. But could we little idiots have been wrong this whole time and called him a derogatory name by mistake? I was cowed and embarrassed. He kept chuckling when he held my hand as we walked together to my room. He wasn't angry, and definitely was not some freakish or mean colossus! He was a strapping and tall local farm boy that now also doubled as a middle-aged janitor. That's all. He nodded to my teacher before briefly opening all the windows and shooing out the unwanted six-legged skunks. Mrs. Hutch…. was happy, my classmates settled down and Mr. M…. left, but not before giving me a wink and a smile. I now knew his real name and was beaming with pride. I could hardly wait to correct my pals or anyone else who messed up that man's last name. He was now my buddy, although quite a large friend at that. Years later, as a young adult, I purchased the Queen album *News of The World* and on the front cover was an image of a robot that was a dead ringer for old Mr. M…. I remember laughing out loud as it easily brought back those second grade memories. Thanks, Mr. M…. for NOT being a monster.

28

Smokes

I wouldn't say I was a particularly precocious child but I could read above grade level and print words rather well. And I was observant of my surroundings, even at age seven. I was also somewhat of an anxious and nervous young man with a nosy personality. Curiosity killed the cat but while not wantonly mischievous or overtly daring, many things in my childhood interested me, and I took notice of them. Case in point: cigarettes. My mother and I had gone shopping together to the Grand Union grocery store on Main Street at least hundreds of times before I even entered second grade. So, it was a no-brainer for me to memorize the two rows of brands in the cigarette vending machine in the foyer of that food market, next to the shopping carts. Sixty-cents got you a pack of smokes, in those days. You dropped in the coins, pulled the knob adjacent to your favorite brand and got your fix. It seemed important to me at the time to remember the cigarette types. I reasoned that I knew a lot of world flags by sight and those were just other important badges that you had to know. Adults smoked, TV ads and billboards promoted it, not to mention all the cigarette and cigar-shaped candy available for kids. It was part of Americana, kind of like knowing the rules of football and baseball. Upon exit from that supermarket one day, even before we got to that cancer-stick dispenser, I chimed up and recited all the brands out loud to my mom. Pall Mall, Virginia Slims, Salem, Benson and Hedges, Camel, Newport, Kool, Kent, Marlboro, True, Lucky Strike, Winston, etc. She stopped, looked at me in horror and said, "Why do you know that? Who taught you about such nasty things?" I thought she was going to slap me to get those evil thoughts out of my head. My proud accomplishment quickly turned sour. She kept on staring at me as she roughly pulled me from the store, still shaking her head at my failing. Now she had to worry about me becoming a smoker later in life. I was crestfallen and assured her nothing like that would ever happen. She berated me all the way home as we walked and SHE talked. Sullenly I listened as she mentioned cancer, that dreaded disease, over and over again. Boy, all that lecturing because of a dang machine. Nevertheless, I suddenly realized that even casual curiosity could kill you. I never picked up the tobacco habit although I did smoke an occasional cigar in adulthood. Mom, thanks for being so vigilant and yelling at me back then.

29

Dinosaurs Galore

It started in kindergarten, then gradually improved and became more complete, finally reaching its zenith in second grade. Kind of a slow progression, like evolution. I am talking about dinosaurs, namely drawing, painting and coloring them. I was a prodigious artist in those early grades, not gifted but slightly talented nonetheless. Miss N., my Kindergarten teacher, saved a lot of my sketches and gave them to my folks years after I graduated from high school. My first grade teacher, Mrs. H. couldn't care less and probably used my detailed and colorful drawings as kindling for her wood stove at home, or to wrap fish in when her inebriated husband wobbled home from a day of ice fishing. However, the very impressed Mrs. Hutch…., in second grade, much appreciated my "realistic" dinosauric expressions on paper. Many was the time when she would hover over my desk and marvel at the quickness and deliberateness of my brontosaurus renderings. I loved all things about those offbeat-looking beasts and thought they were a *neat* group of prehistoric animals. Stegosaurus, triceratops, T-Rex, ankylosaurus, dimetrodon and others were on my palate and in my wheelhouse of limited creative skill. While others in my class drew rocks and stick figures, I stuck with my obsession. My fellow artsy classmates knew it was my *bag* and they also enjoyed looking at the finished products. To be honest, I didn't draw much else that second year. And I always smiled whenever we drove out of town and went past the long defunct, one pump, Sinclair gasoline station near the outskirts of our village. The faded logo still had a green Brontosaurus painted on it. Fossil fuel! Oh well, my artistic Jurassic interpretations had had a good run. We didn't have much time for pencil-and-paper art in third grade; I'm glad I got it out of my system in second grade, so to speak.

30

Timing is Everything

Many of my classmates and I could sort of tell the time by second grade, mostly intuitively, by living it. However, you had to be specific to prove to elderly Mrs. Hutch.... that you actually comprehended what the big hand (hours) and little hand (minutes) stood for and to accurately express the time, at that moment. There was no second hand to worry about, however. And no guessing, sun watching, or shadow spotting allowed! You had to learn to love that white orb with long black needles on it and what it was trying to tell you. It was hard at first. I always got the easy ones right; you know, six o'clock, three o'clock.... But what about thirty-six minutes after one p.m.? That was a toughie, at least for me. The whole concept vaguely resembled playing darts. You had to instantly know where a particular number was before throwing at it. It was much the same with clock watching. Mrs. Hutch.... wanted us to quickly, and with certainty, know the time by forcing us daily to memorize that darn clock face and its black mustache, one that kept changing shape. After lunch and recess, but no nap time, she would test us. She had us take out a lined sheet of paper, walk through the rows with a clock stamp, stamp each of our papers six times and then walk to the front of the room. Then she would tell us six different clock positions she wanted drawn on the six numbered faces on our paper. Ten minutes after four, 9:16, twelve o'clock, etc. We printed our names in the top right corners of the papers and handed them in. When every single person got at least five out of six right, she relented in that daily barrage of timeliness and quizzed us weekly instead. I learned to tell the time, thanks to Mrs. Hutch…. And, whenever a classmate would ask me what the clock said, I would invariably retort, "It doesn't say anything, you have to look at it." Duh.

31

The Big Bruiser

My parents had always assumed that I became afflicted
with fall hay fever because of an encounter with "raw" hay
in a neighbor's barn when I was almost five years old, and
just about to enter kindergarten. But then, after numerous
visits (five bucks a pop) to Dr. K., he gently reassured my
folks that my seasonal allergy, including the watery red
eyes, runny nose, sneezing and coughing, was not from
exposure to hay but to local ragweed. Some people were
susceptible and most were not. Lucky me. So, every
autumn for the next two years I wept, sniffled and
sputtered until November. I probably could have taken the
primitive antihistamines at the time but I forgot that my
parents behaved like Christian Scientists when it came to
medications. And they were NOT Christian Scientists! At
last my father had had enough with his son looking like a
sniveling piece of crap every fall. Upon consultation with
Dr. K. (another five dollars), an appointment was made
with an ENT specialist at a nearby surgical hospital to see
if removing my tonsils and adenoids would help. I was a
scrawny, sickly looking child in second grade; anything
would have helped at that point. I often had trouble

breathing through my nose and had a piss-poor appetite. The specialist consultation went badly, however. You see, the Christmas before, I had received my best present to date: a large, white-colored, battery-operated and steerable tow truck toy, complete with flashing lights and realistic sounds. It was a beauty. I played with that two-foot-long, four-wheeled toy practically nonstop. It gobbled up batteries at an alarming rate but I managed to keep it alive by begging and borrowing D-cells from family members. It was called The Big Bruiser. As I sat nervously and nearly naked on the ENT's chilly examination table, he matter-of-factly asked me directly if I had any bruises on my body, I guess to check for a possible bleeding or clotting disorder prior to surgery. I mistakenly thought he was speaking of my popular toy at home and proudly announced, "Yes, I have a big bruiser." He squinted at me, appeared quite alarmed, and asked, "Where, show me?" Quizzically, I glanced at my father in the room and retorted, "It's at my house, in my family room." The doctor looked confused, as I was. My father was mum, as usual. The ENT specialist shook his head and silently examined every inch of me very carefully and most likely assumed that there was a language barrier of some sort in that room. I had the operation but only had my adenoid glands removed. The surgeon told my pop that my tonsils were fine and could stay put. After a tasty overnight stay in the hospital recovery room, eating all the Jell-O and ice cream I could stand, I was discharged and went home. And guess what? I could breathe again, and through my nose. And a slender and starved-looking child started to immediately put on weight after that surgical procedure. It had been a timely and successful medical diagnosis and my parents were extremely pleased with the profound results. Their boy was coming back to life. Forty years hence I found out that my seasonal rhinitis was actually caused by a type of alfalfa grass, grown in Kansas, whose spring pollen slowly made its way eastward and made me sneeze every fall. The local ragweed was innocent in my case. And guess what else? My invulnerable and "illness immune" father developed springtime allergies in his late forties. He was annoyed and angry when told by old Dr. K. (another five dollars, please) that it can happen sometimes, even in the best of families.

32

The Dreaded Backswing

I was voluntarily *drafted* by some older male children to
play "backyard" baseball almost nightly that hot summer,
after my second grade year had ended. I could catch,
throw and run rather well for my age but they only wanted
me as a permanent catcher, a glorified backstop. I would
be catching for both teams. No batting, no running and
no playing, just catching. But I didn't care. It was an
honor to play sports with the "big" kids on the block. To
them I was an enthusiastic baseball sucker, that's all. No
gloves were used and the pitcher threw underhanded, so
the baseball velocity was somewhat muted during play.
The modified and shortened baseball field was at
Chapman's, an adjacent neighbor's gnarly yard. I caught
the pitches that weren't hit and dutifully threw the balls
back to the "mound." I could even snag wayward thrown
balls; both teams liked having me there, I think. However,
I was the youngest boy present at seven years of age; the
thirteen and fourteen-year-olds were twice my age and
some of them, twice my height! But then it happened: the
unthinkable. My Mom's worst nightmare materialized. In
her doorway stood her handsome Izzy, now battered,

bruised and bloodied, and bawling his head off. I had a puffy and bloody upper lip and mangled upper front teeth. I was a crying mess. My Mom quickly got me cleaned up with a wet washcloth, applied another cold cloth to my face as a compress, and stormed out of our house leaving me standing there, still sobbing. She literally ran down to the playing field to confront the older boys and find out what had happened to her darling little boy. Although usually soft-spoken and demure, she loudly berated them for not watching out for me. One smart aleck came forward to tell her that I had foolishly stepped forward into his practice backswing and got whacked. Mom glared at him and forcibly confiscated his bat. He should have known better than to offer resistance against an angry mom. I now had a free bat. That evening my dad surprisingly said nothing as he took me to Dr. K, our family physician, while my mom stayed home with my toddler sister. The doctor said my baby teeth would turn black and soon fall out. My lip was cut badly but did not require stitches. He turned out to be correct with both diagnoses. We never made it over to see Old Doc Smithe, the only town dentist that was sober, sane and competent. Well, I did visit him after a few months' time, when my permanent front adult teeth started growing in. My mom wanted to double-check to make sure they were undamaged. Doc Smithe assured her that my new choppers were intact and not to worry. We all started to see him for regular dental cleaning/checkup appointments after my unexpected oral altercation; another doctor to add to our health care team. A dentist, good grief. And no one played baseball again next door after that dustup with my old lady, even though the immediate neighbors knew that we were moving up the street that summer. She could be a toughie, if need be.

33

A Budding Naturalist

Although I caught the bug early, literally speaking, I did not fervently begin scouring backyards, fields and streams for all winged things and slimy creepie-crawlies until age seven. It was a super safe neighborhood, virtually devoid of traffic, a haven of old homes and widows, on a quiet boulevard called Clinton Street. My family and I had just moved up the street from one rental abode to another, this time to a small house in back of the landlady's home which faced the street. My mother had gotten my passion boiling the previous two years, while living at our first rental apartment, taking me across the wide street and introducing me to the narrow brook behind the First Presbyterian Church. They were supposed to be relaxing nature walks but quickly morphed into frenzied animal collecting missions on my part. However, I was very young and couldn't go by myself. But now, being two years older, braver, and very familiar with my surroundings, I would grab my homemade butterfly net, a few empty envelopes, an old spaghetti strainer, and a small bucket and then traverse my expansive habitat. Although it wasn't to be different. I HAD to do it. What made other people squeamish and grossed out was normal behavior for me. All the kindly widows knew me, in fact I probably provided them with a jolt of life at times. Seeing a young lad running through their backyards chasing a tiger swallowtail butterfly must have been an unusual sight for a usually dour and quiet residential street. I had permission to trespass at will through adjoining yards, and had the locations of vegetable gardens, delicate flower berms and ditches memorized so as not to stumble as I dashed about. I was a lowly second grader living in that area, had one immediate friend my age (N.K.) on that road, and let nature be my new bosom buddy. My former city friends were a distant faded memory now and I truly did not miss them. I would dip in and out of the mowed properties and then jump down the bordering embankments to check out the brook for spiders and salamanders. The strainer was to help me catch mudpuppies with, the bucket to store them in. And the envelopes? They were for keeping freshly caught butterflies, with wings neatly folded, until I reached home. I liked being seven in the summertime, on that street, in my new town, free to explore, wonder, imagine, and collect. It was a special, carefree and joyous time for me. My Grandpa Pete had recently moved in with us and his horns, and true colors, didn't show yet. More of that story will be told later. Suffice it to say that my entomological and amphibious leanings were greatly curtailed by him as I grew older. But for now, I was a free-range intrepid bug hunter and salamander sleuth, and loved it.

34

Return of the Patriarchy

My mom always knew it would happen, it was inevitable. She had had a few good years in the boondocks after our escape from the "overlord" in the city, and boy was she grateful, as I heard her tell my father, over and over again. However, it was only a matter of time until the "good times" ended. He was a 65-year-old widower now, recently retired, and, didn't wish to be alone. He needed people to direct and boss around. He was suddenly a king without a fiefdom. My Grandpa Pete sold his house and unceremoniously moved in with us in 1967. Forget about *old school*, he was *old world*, from the *old country*. My father and I were both in class all day, he as a college professor, and I in second grade. My sister was a toddler-head, just above an ankle biter, and innocently clueless. That left my housewife-mom and grandpa cooped up in a tiny rental home, all day long, getting on each others' nerves. I won't bore you with details of the arguments, discord and petty bullshit that accompanied disparate in-laws living together. Even after we moved into our newly built home in '69, and even with his own spacious first floor bedroom, the "general" was unrequited, and continually stirred up trouble in our new household. Sure, he was unjustly persecuted during the war, lost all his vast land holdings and riches and barely made it to the U.S. with his wife and son, my dad. I had heard all his gut-wrenching and melancholy stories hundreds of times. He still feared the Russians would come for him, years later. A form of PTSD may have dogged him, who knows? But every WWII immigrant had a story. Spontaneous and unbridled joy was once again basically banned from our lives, although I did catch HIM enjoying *All in the Family* and *Sanford and Son*, on TV on a regular basis. Fortunately, a constant array of weekend *projects* and a gargantuan garden of his own design kept him occupied during the summer months; the wintertime, however, was brutal on my mom. In 1975 she escaped again, this time into higher education. What? At middle age she enrolled and graduated with honors from the two-year junior college in town, eating lunch daily with my pop in his office. Then she gained a B.S. and M.S. in languages from a neighboring university. Then, by 1987, she began teaching French and Spanish in earnest, as a full-time professor in the same college as my father! Who knew she had it in her? Who knew that she was so good at languages? My "doormat" mom? Holy moly! I was long gone into higher education and married, as was my sister, but kept hearing that our former household relationships had greatly improved. There was a loose truce between the combatants and newfound respect for my mother from my dad AND grandpa. In hindsight, my grandfather, who lived to be 99, balanced out his derogatory ways with solid help on the home front. He fixed cars, greatly contributed to the building of our home, did odd jobs, ran the yearly bountiful garden, and could fix about anything. This saved our family lots of money over the years. He even lent his tough body to build my own house years later, and my sister's, as well. He was 92 years old and slung roofing shingles around like they were feathers. On the downside, he greatly impaired my relationship with my father, often belittling me as a lowly subordinate sissy instead of as a bona fide and intelligent grandson. My sister "got it" from him just as badly. And early on he damaged any chance of a loving father-in-law relationship with my mom. But, strangely, the world did not end as he predicted it would upon his passing. Somehow we soldiered on without him. Glory be. Although his rough hands and rough persona often rode roughshod over us, all the while bullying we "weak" family members, I have to admit that he instilled a dynamic work ethic in my sister and me, and we continue to begrudgingly remember him. And I became somewhat of a rebellious comic at heart, probably in self-defense, all those decades ago. What more of a legacy can one leave?

35

Punching Bag

My "best friend" in second grade was in my immediate class and would be a neighbor in the distant future. But for now, P.R. was seven years old, like me. Tow-headed, blue-eyed and rough-cut, a polar opposite of yours truly. He did have an ounce of brain, however. We grew into becoming pals, at least at the beginning of the school year. Our mothers, however, had to grin and bear our camaraderie. They had nothing in common. Our fathers were also from two disparate worlds. Mine was an astute Estonian immigrant, a former city kid and now a college professor in town. His, a cigar-chomping, redneck, good ole' boy, and lifelong townie, driving an oil truck for a living. Incredibly, they bonded for life over pistol-team shooting, guns, ammo, hunting and fishing. Weird but true. As I already mentioned, P.R. and I hit it off at the beginning. But by the end of the school year he was regularly hitting me! And not just play fighting as boys do sometimes. I had somehow become his personal punching bag at the morning communal bus stop on my street. Only kids were there, without any adult supervision. What the hell had happened between us? I was clueless and distraught. As a hard-wired anxious child, I was keyed up on most days anyway. I didn't need to feel even more miserable. This unwarranted behavior continued sporadically and we no longer spoke to one another or sat on the bus together. I ended up sitting next to his younger sister who was nice to me. Eventually I grew weary and sore of getting gut-punched out of the blue at 7:30 a.m. and finally told my parents. They went ballistic. My mom immediately marched over to P.R.'s house and confronted his mother, L. Now, my mom was usually a quiet, dignified, and nonaggressive, woman. Well, as she told the story, she had it out verbally with the miscreant's mom but got nowhere fast. P.R.'s mom dismissed the whole bullying fiasco as boys being boys and said that if I wasn't tough enough then it was my own fault. Then my mother mentioned what would happen if I fought back and hurt her son? L. shrugged, lit a cigarette and arrogantly said that she doubted anyone could best her son in a fight and she wasn't worried. My mom left in a huff. This left my old man to take care of things. He was outraged as he confronted P.R.'s old man, his friend, who stood a head shorter than he. My pop was a terrific athlete and had been in many scrapes himself as a youth. Nobody wanted a piece of him, either on the tennis court or in the college classroom. He could make a thug turn tail in a hurry.

Things were immediately smoothed over without any fisticuffs betwixt the parental males and we agreed to keep buying fuel oil from them. But just to be on the safe side, for my benefit, my paternal grandfather, who now lived with us, would sometimes follow me to the bus stop at a distance and keep watch over things. P.R. and the other children knew who he was. He didn't fool anyone with his presence but P.R. had already stopped his abuse of me by then. End of story, or not? P.R. got a second wind by sixth grade to pick up where he left off and started in on me again. I don't know why. His periodic sneak attacks were disturbing and seemed to occur after recess as we were walking back to our classes. Always a hard sucker punch in the back and a quick exit was his style. He never got caught by any teachers present. But he got his just desserts before the year ended and my paranoia subsided. That succeeding outbreak of his antipathy toward me will be discussed in a future vignette. Suffice it to say that P.R. lasted until the eighth grade, grew his blond locks out, became infamous as an illicit drug supplier and user, and left school. He was just too *cool* to be constrained by academia. He raised truancy and juvenile delinquency to an elegant and deviant art form. Everyone in town knew he was a waste case but no one intervened. His love life also became a big mess. I left town for a college education.

He capitulated and took the easy townie route, took over for his father and continued to deliver fuel oil to my parents' house. Gone was the hair, the swashbuckling bombast, and the unjustified antagonism toward our family. And I don't believe he called my folks "dirty Russians" anymore. He became a soft-spoken, portly, and polite man who whispered demurely to my mother whilst filling up their fuel tanks. My mom and his mom continued to just barely tolerate each other. However, my pop and his pop remained friends for life. And me? If I ever run into him again, it will not be *pretty* for him. But I haven't seen him in over 50 years, so we are both safe, for now.

36

Kindred Spirits

It all happened so quickly, and serendipitously. One minute I was lurking in his backyard and searching for black swallowtail caterpillars on his garden carrot tops and in the next, HE was standing over me, demanding an explanation for my trespassing temerity. He wasn't that tall, but I was only seven, so any adult was bigger than me. He was a little portly, however. Anyway, in a gruff tone, he brayed, "What are you doing in my garden, causing mischief?" I recoiled and started to stammer apologetically. Didn't this neighbor get the memo? Didn't he realize that I had carte blanche to run amok in the neighborhood backyards while hunting for arthropods and other critters? I had seen him many times before but we had never exchanged syllables. Not even a friendly hello. He lived barely one house up from me so I figured I could cut through my own backyard and through his on the way to old Miss Hayes' yard, where her tons of colored flowers attracted a butt load of butterflies. I was obviously mistaken as he glared down at me. Before I could back away he beckoned me into his house, and even held the door open so I could enter first. What could I do? If I resisted, maybe he would call my mom and report me. Perhaps even call the police? I quickly accepted his stern demand and sullenly and dejectedly walked into the house. As the door slammed shut behind me I looked around and almost cried out. There, on all the walls, hung frames and frames of mounted butterflies, some of which I had never seen locally before. I finally blinked as I took in the rows of insect volumes lining his bookshelves and then heard booming laughter behind me. Dr. C. R. was a long retired Presbyterian minister in our town and the local authority on Lepidoptera (butterflies). He told me that he had heard of my existence and could hardly wait to "capture" me and train me up the right way. No more being an "amateur," running hither and tither on the loose, haphazardly looking for insects. And I thought I was a successful bug hunter, with salamanders thrown in for good measure. This guy was serious. He proceeded to sit me down and gave me a crash course in entomology on that Sunday afternoon. His two dogs, Tippy and Buffy, which I already knew well, came by, sniffed me, and left. His wife interrupted us a few times to try to extricate me from his "sermon," but he shooed her away and said flatly that I had many things to learn and he was just getting started. He was sixty-plus years my senior and desperately wanted to pass on his deep love of entomology to me. I instinctively realized that I was blessed to have him as a nearby neighbor and future mentor. Well, two lemonades and a box of cookies later, he showed me the door and asked me how I felt about being *educated* by him? I smiled coyly and promised to return the following weekend and excitedly ran home to tell my mom. But, NOT my dad. Thus began an unplanned, years-long apprenticeship with the benevolent Dr. R., who was actually a nice old pastor and whom I would dutifully and regularly visit while on my *rounds* in the area. He taught me a multitude of "important things" that very summer; mainly a scientific approach to collecting and mounting specimens, specifically butterflies. I needed a small notebook, a few choice *Peterson Field Guide to Butterflies* books, a proper butterfly net, and a willingness to learn all I could from the *Master*, him. The notebook was to jot down the name, location and date of insect capture, the field guides were to properly identify the species caught. He bought me a genuine butterfly net from an entomological supply house and I was greatly appreciative. The *Peterson Field Guides* were purchased at the bookstore section in a nearby city that my family frequently visited. I was all set. But all this pressure, could I handle it? I had just passed second grade, dang it. I wanted to relax in the summer and have fun MY way, and here was this bellicose old timer badgering me to live up to HIS standards of amateur entomology. However, I loved it. He taught me how to carefully kill butterflies with a quick pinch of the thorax, how to precisely cut off the wings, attach them to fake paper bodies, and mount them in glass frames with previously dyed flowers and colorful tissue paper as background. I also mounted many whole, with a pin, in plastic containers or cigar boxes, complete with affixed labels, after using his stretching board: professional grade, baby! I was learning fast. I also had jars upon jars of caterpillars, munching leaves, pooping and pupating on my porch. Not to mention the praying mantids, walkingstick insects, dragonfly nymphs and two-lined salamanders that also were captives of mine. Everyone ate well, though. No one starved. Late summer was approaching and milkweed-loving monarchs were everywhere. But whenever we discussed them, he pronounced them *Monriks*. That's how I heard it, anyway. This went on for a few weeks before I had to ask his wife if we were talking about the same butterfly. She laughed and said yes. He had a slight New England accent and sometimes *monarch* sounded like *monrik*. One day I sauntered over to his house and saw another car parked behind his early sixties, eggplant color, two-door Pontiac Tempest. I parked my new net at his back door, looked inside, saw people talking, and started to leave when Mrs. R. suddenly ushered me in. I didn't want to be rude and bug him if he had company. However, I was invited and ran inside in a flash, and then chuckled to myself to see my no-nonsense, karate-trained, K-3 school gym teacher, Mr. B. Mac., talking "butterflies" to Doctor R. They turned to acknowledge my presence and Mr. Mac. turned beet red, in embarrassment I presumed. We knew each other, and now I knew his "secret." An ex-marine and all-around tough guy, he was not a cross-dresser, he was worse, he was INTO butterflies. What a wussy! Ha, ha. Wait a minute, so was I. Needless to say, when third grade commenced that fall, he gave me that knowing look the first day of gym, and my high marks in his class reflected a desire to keep his hobby under wraps, and to keep my trap shut. Hey, his secret was safe with me. I flaunted my passion, but he, obviously, did not. I NEVER tattled on him; I enjoyed receiving high grades, although as a developing athlete myself I probably deserved them anyway. My relationship with Dr. R. continued after we moved away into our new home. Habitually, I would come down the hill to visit him even though I now had my own big backyard to sweep for specimens. I also frequented the brook to get my fill of aquatic wildlife and would casually stroll over to his place, always as a welcome guest and *student*. By sixth grade my sojourns to Clinton

Street grew less and less. My father and Grandpa Pete, although at first marveling at my pastime, thought I would have outgrown it by now and started to worry that I was wrongfully maturing as a delinquent "nature boy" instead of as a serious-minded, future civil engineer or doctor. I heard the many anguished arguments in my household and felt terribly that I was letting down my old man. Grandpa Pete was always fond of remarking, "When I was your age, I was single-handedly plowing fields on my Estonian farm, while managing two unruly horses. You will never amount to anything if you don't grow up." As a result, my free time was purposely cut into to do "manly" projects and chores around the house. That supposedly was to teach me responsibility and knock that naturalism crap out of my head. It hurt. That forced me to deftly sneak away as often as possible to continue my naughty habit. I think smoking a few Lucky Strikes would have been more readily accepted by my family. Zoology definitely was not. At least not anymore. The last time Dr. R. and I interacted was when I started seventh grade. To be honest, I was also actively practicing and competing in piano, tennis and table tennis by then; my bug catching days were growing short. Be that as it may, he had taught me so much and I am forever grateful. I passed on all I knew to my brilliant and athletic firstborn, my daughter; she must have been genetically predisposed as well because she earned a B.Sc. degree in Applied Zoology and a Ph.D. in Ecology and Evolutionary Biology. I never squelched her zeal, passion or zoological momentum, and I revel in her continued determination for success in her chosen field.

37

The Dog Days of Summer

Yes, it is a common saying, one describing the long, hot days of late summer; however, this vignette is really about dogs. Clinton Street was a spectacular and most special street to me. It was wide, long and replete with old, stately maple trees lining the edges, next to the large homes and slate sidewalks. As I had no furry or "store-bought" pets, I "adopted" many of the local dogs. Not cats, just dogs. Tippy and Buffy lived two houses up from me. They were border collies and resided at Dr. R.'s home. I played with them whenever I visited him to bone up on entomological knowledge. Then there was Rebel, the oversized, snarling, white-haired German shepherd that would swoop down the street and run over to me to be played with. He was really a sweetie, however. And Shotze, a large, tan colored lab-mix that came over from nearby Cross Street and loved to be bellyrubbed. King was an obnoxious and foul tempered dachshund, owned by our new landlady, Mrs. Young. He would sometimes bite her. I stayed away from that darn *dawg*. Pumpkin was a playful pup at the top of the street and liked to be petted frontwards and backwards, with and against the grain! Freckles was a naughty spotted canine; he would sometimes gently but maliciously nudge over the multiple glass jars of praying mantids that lined my porch to get at the specks of raw hamburger meat inside. He had a good nose but his reward was miniscule at best. All those dogs were collared, had a unique personality, and each was free to roam around during the day. Nobody complained, except if maybe they left a stinky *pile* in someone's yard, that is. But for the most part, Clinton Street was their territory, and I was a good friend. I got my fill of dog ownership without actually possessing one, and I never begged my folks for one. I already had a plethora of four-AND six-legged surrogate companions to take care of, including salamanders, mudpuppies, caterpillars and mantids. However, they were unappreciative of petting and couldn't roll over on command. Just sayin.'

38

The Haunted Mansion

My father bought a "haunted" mansion! How cool was that? Frankly speaking, however, it was the only house "available" to we *outsiders* at the time. Additionally, my pop wanted a home in town, close to the college where he was a professor, plus within walking distance to the high school and stores. When I saw it for the first time my mouth fell open as I gazed in wonderment. It instantly reminded me of the Addams' and Munsters' homes on those seminal TV comedy shows. Was this really going to be our dwelling, to live in? For real? Could my "genius" dad resurrect it? Here's the story: My family and I were quite excited to move to a new home and leave the rental world behind. It turned out, however, to be an excruciating and unpleasant ordeal for my father. He was the one that did all the legwork, convincing the offering party to sell to him and fending off other would-be buyers. It wasn't easy. It was a labor of love, but finally we would get our dream house. However, it wasn't without controversy. We had been renting for four years thus far, in three different houses, on the same street. Plus I now had a baby sister and my paternal grandfather as extra family members. We needed more room. It was time to move on. Pop came home one night from a "late meeting" and informed us that after much wrangling and perceived animosity, he did indeed purchase that dilapidated "haunted" house on the dead-end street, up on the hill, overlooking the village. A real "haunted" house? Are you kidding? The property deed had fallen into the Episcopal Church's hands years before, after decades of neglect and no human habitation. In the early 1800s, the house was a grand Victorian abode with two majestic turrets, huge porches, many side buildings, and an ornate outhouse. It also contained very primitive electricity and plumbing. Structurally it was unsound but had a unique history that many people in our town still fondly, though warily, remembered. Many townies had trespassed on the property and *lifted* things from that house for years, all the while keeping a lookout for alleged apparitions. It was an eyesore although a source of local legend and lore. No one wanted things changed and local folks actually believed that the right buyer would restore that monstrosity back to its former glory days. Being a civil engineer and architect by training, my dad had other ideas. As he showed us the deed that fateful night, he said that he had to fend off many other prospective buyers in the process. It turned out that the property would have been purchased long ago except for the fact that there was an active water spring in the basement that flooded the cellar, no septic system, poor plumbing, and possibly paranormal activity in the attic. Most would-be builders/buyers were looking to refurbish it somehow, but didn't know where to begin. And those scary spooks.... Anyhow, upon buying the lot, my pop quickly surveyed the land, drew up the blueprints himself, sketched the house out on paper, and applied for the appropriate building permits. Many visits to that house by my family occurred that spring. I remember walking gingerly through the dingy and dimly lit rooms. It was old and stinky. I had to watch out for the holes in the floors, the broken glass, and the filth. The rotten wood odor almost knocked me down. I searched for the suspected ghastly spirits but was disappointed. None materialized for me. The house could not be saved. On a warm summer's day in 1967, in a bold and blasphemous move, my old man had contractors put a chain around the existing structure, gave the bulldozer operator the signal, and had it torn down, in one fell swoop. Neighbors and onlookers gasped and started to weep, the police were summoned. Such sacrilege! How dare he tear down a "landmark" home, and why didn't "they" think of it first? My dad scoffed at the *kibitzers* and sarcastically informed all those within earshot that it was the only way to get rid of the ghosts. Many of the village idiots actually believed him. He continued with the demolition until nothing stood upright. Gone was the house, the rotted sheds and that crumbling outhouse. Some of the skeptical parties present were not aware of his skills and thought that we "Russian foreigners" were just going to wing it. How wrong they were. My Grandpa P. and father had managed to tame the property and the natives at once, terraced the land, rerouted that cellar spring water, and began to dig out a proper hole for our new domicile. Then winter set in and all building ceased. Townspeople didn't know what to make of the project. The old mansion was gone, and the supposed malevolent phantoms banished. I had already started third grade, and we were ready to continue our labors in earnest the following spring. We were on OUR schedule, not that of the natives.

39

Refugee Camping

Just when I thought I had the old man figured out, he
fooled me again. I have already alluded to the fact that he
was a demanding drillmaster, a perfectionist, a civil
engineering professor, all-around gifted athlete, gunsmith,
and horologist. I always felt so inadequate and inferior
around him. Coupled with my *old-school*, workaholic,
live-in paternal grandfather, I accepted my miserable fate as
an inconsequential peon and lowly *putz*. However, who
knew that my pop liked vacations? Real ones, not just the
three months he had off from teaching every summer. And
who knew that he liked the ocean? Nobody had ever
discussed such blasphemy before in our nose-to-the-
grindstone, "immigrant-minded" family. He started
planning on taking my mom, me and my baby sister on a
trip to the seashore that late summer in '67, but where?
He had no clue but was busy studying maps and talking
outloud about distances and other states. Other states? It
began to sound auspicious to a rising third-grader. In late
August, as I came home one afternoon after a tough outing
chasing tiger swallowtail butterflies, my dad laid it on us.
My always scowling and scolding Grandpa Pete would be

staying home (thank goodness) while we four would drive to Connecticut the next day and search out the ocean. Wow! My conservative father had been serious about this trip after all. But it was going to be a weekend affair only, no reservations had been made, or anything resembling a "normally" plotted vacation. I had forgotten that my parents were selectively phone phobic, restaurant/lodging-shy, and rarely asked for help or directions in life. But it was a chance to get away from our town and Grandpa Pete. I was excited. Mom busily packed food and provisions as if Connecticut was the 1880's Wild West, without grocery stores or ANY amenities. Saturday morning came and we embarked on our expedition inside our trusty Oldsmobile station wagon. So we drove, and drove some more. Those were the days before major turnpikes had been completed. No rest areas, no nothing, just small towns and endless driving. Six hours later we were in New Haven, in the state of Connecticut, and in a state of euphoric shock. We had made it. Bring on the water! Dad had figured out that the nearest seashore to us was Long Island Sound, on the Connecticut side. Not New Jersey, not southern New York State, but the "Nutmeg State." We were all set now. Driving east along Route 1, dad assumed there would be plenty of beach access pull-offs to satisfy our lust for sand and salty water.

We could then park, relax, swim and have fun. That was how Florida had been for my folks when they had visited it, many, many years prior. Lots of sandy beach and loads of places to pull over and recreate. Not so in the "Constitution State," however. By late evening we dejectedly stopped at a Mobil station for gas, rest and, relief. We were halfway up the coast and had not yet seen any water. But the gas station attendant struck up a fortuitous conversation with my dad and told him about state parks ahead, very near the road we were currently on; especially one that kissed the sea. Our enthusiasm returned as we bedded down for the night in an old abandoned warehouse parking lot with a gorgeous view of a drive-in movie playing on a large screen. Of course there was no sound, but it was a Bob Hope, Phyllis Diller screwball comedy flick and no sound was necessary to figure out the gist of the movie. My sister and I slept uncomfortably in the back while my parents dozed in the front seats of the car. Bright and early the next morning, pop loudly announced that we were turning into a campground called Hammonasset Beach State Park, just as my sister and I were awakening from our slumber in the car. Were we in Indian country? Was I dreaming? Was my father pronouncing that name correctly? I rubbed my eyes and saw the signs for myself at the entrance. That was the name all right. We had no camping equipment but for a nominal fee were let in as visitors and directed toward the visitor parking lot. Dad slowly drove past the six hundred or so oceanic campsites on the way to park the car and remarked how close to the seashore we were. We had struck gold. Well, after a day of sun and fun, near a huge oceanfront pavilion at which we bought hot dogs and French fries, it was unanimously decided that we most definitely would return next summer as bona fide campers, and stay longer. Never mind that my mom had gotten a sunburn or that I had swum headfirst into a submerged pink jellyfish or that my sister had mildly cut her toe on a hermit crab shell. But it was all in good fun. The ride home went by quickly with nonstop banter about our future return trip. My father's rich relative in Indiana was involved in the R.V. business and procured a new, Phoenix pop-up camper for us at cost, which we stored in our newly built garage in the spring of '68. And, after buying tons of obligatory camping equipment, we made the same voyage that summer again and had a riot, this time staying for a week. Never mind that the camping lots had no hookups, were exceedingly small, and had communal bathrooms with cold showers. The place was shabby but we loved it. We were now official campers and knew how to operate a Coleman stove, set up a screen house, and go ocean fishing for the plentiful bluefish and striped bass off the two available rocky jetties. My father seemed a changed man during succeeding late summers. He relished the challenge of towing a swaying camper and looked forward greatly to doing it again and again. Was it our last sojourn as a tight-knit nuclear family? NO! It was the beginning of a 50-plus years adventurous odyssey of regular and compulsory summer camping at our "second home." Then, midway, the camper was sold and a large, new 1976 Coachmen trailer bought and the saga continued. My sister and I literally grew up there. We had the place memorized. It was our special two weeks of bonding with our folks, through sunshine and rain, through family stories and playing Flinch (Parker Bros. card game), dominoes and bingo, through good and bad fishing years. Listening to Queen's, The Eagle's, and Elton John's new hits as well as 1010 WINS AM Radio became the norm in late summer. Hammonasset Beach and the excellent seafood bonanza at the adjacent Lenny and Joe's Fish Tale Restaurant became fond memories, etched into my mind forever. And not just for me and my immediate family. My girlfriend and future wife was invited to come with us in 1980. Now here was a mountain girl that only knew "camping" as a sleeping bag-enveloped and unwashed experience, deep in the Adirondack mountains, devoid of humans, toiletries and basic needs, with dangerous animals shuffling and sniffing about during the nights. When we arrived at Hammonasset Beach, she astonishingly remarked, "this is refugee camping," as she surveyed the hundreds of tents and trailers set up neatly in rows on either side of narrow streets. My father was insulted; this was the only camping he had known and was puzzled at her flippant comment. I managed to smooth over her initial audacious-sounding salvo and we got down to camping, sunning, swimming, and fishing. Fast forward a few years and you know what happened: My wife, and now OUR children, and my parents were still going camping there, with a few more tents added to the experience. My wife had graciously, and long ago, accepted our annual family tradition of "refugee camping" and now our own kids, as well as my sister's family, were growing up there. The park had changed radically over the decades with hot water added, new beach pavilions built, cleanliness as a new priority, and regular patrols added to keep order and to keep out the riffraff. In the '70s, VW Micro-buses full of troublemaking, pot smoking hippies would descend on the park; but no more. It morphed into a gorgeous, family oriented, G-rated campground. The fees had gone up over time but the increases were well worth the price of admission. However, my mom and dad got old, their trailer was sadly donated, and our wondrous yearly summer sojourns finally ended. Recently, though, my grown daughter, her husband, my wife and son made a day-trip to our familiar haunt. It only took three-and-one-half hours thanks to the major thruways now in existence. We told old stories and reminisced as we took in the new nature center building, the same murky, jellyfish infested ocean water, the same jetties that were now devoid of any fish, and we marveled at how things had changed but remained the same. We had our mandatory strawberry shortcake ice creams from the camp store and played Frisbee on the beach before dining at Lenny and Joe's for the umpteenth time. We departed and went our separate ways (my daughter is now a Connecticut girl), spent and satisfied, with whole belly and steamer clams in our bellies. "Refugee camping" was fun after all, if only as a one-day excursion. We will be back, I promise.

Take a break!

THIRD GRADE

40

B.S.

Yes, those were his initials, honestly, and not the tone of
this story. Well some of it may seem unbelievable, but here
goes: In a nutshell, there once lived a family in our town
that were misfits; intellectually, socially and functionally.
Being from the wrong side of the tracks was an
understatement in this case. Are you kidding me? If you
crossed those defunct train tracks and the covered wooden
bridge at the north end of our village you would literally
run into B.S.'s rundown, ramshackle of an abode, complete
with a broken down doghouse and worn looking outhouse
in the backyard. His family lived in a Depression era style,
but this was the mid-1960s! There were loose boards and
planks strewn everywhere, holes in the roof, a chicken coop
near the front steps, no lawn, no driveway, broken
windows, etc. A mess of a domicile. There was no car.
Evidently a seemingly chaotic homestead translated into a
chaotic life for young B.S. as well. He was 14 and in the
third grade with me, in my class. The elementary school
didn't know what to do or where to put him. It's as if they
were babysitting him until he left on his own volition,
which is what eventually transpired. I recall him looking

like he just fell out of a tree, wearing filthy, high-water pants, and suspenders. He had that spooked, fearful, wild look in his eyes, as if he was going to fight for his life at any time. Comparatively, the rest of us short statured third graders were meek and mild. He was full of homespun wisdom but dumb as a box of rocks. He could barely read and write. He was already knackered and ready for the dustbin of life. But why? Was it the obvious poverty, genetics, nature-nurture garbage? It was an unreal scene and situation. If you were to peek into our class at the time, you would have certainly noticed a six-foot tall man sitting awkwardly behind a tiny desk with erect posture while the majority of the class appeared rather blandly homogenous. Was he a different species from the rest? And his sordid tales of being continuously punished by a dysfunctional father made us cringe in empathy and sympathy for him. And he wasn't a Mormon, a Jehovah's Witness, Born Again Christian Fundamentalist, Amish, or from the Ozarks. Or was he? Perhaps abject poverty, squalor and mental instability could have caused some of his bizarre symptoms as some of us eight-year-olds surmised. B.S. had started in kindergarten but this was his first class with me. I sat directly behind him, next to the blackboard. I could barely see the teacher because he was so big. Why was this hokey idiot in my room? Wasn't

Special Ed the place for him? Although somewhat dimwitted, he would often utter the following phrase, as if to demonstrate that he meant business being in school: "If I don't larn me some readin' and writin' my pappy done gonna give me a lickin' for sure." Who talked like that? Come on. This wasn't the poor South of yesteryear. But he left before the rest of us moved to fourth grade in the big building the following September. I guess he had all the book learning, reading and writing that he needed or could handle. I heard that the whole damn family had left town in a hurry and abandoned their junk heap. Many years later, as I would ride my ten-speed past his horrible and condemned house, I would silently wonder if he was still alive and remembered that shy little dark-haired and dark-skinned boy that sat behind him who did NOT tease him while funning everyone else in class. The evolving class clown and B.S. were actually pals, and always will be. I admit to having romanticized our strange friendship somewhat. However, one day as I related this story to my dad back then, he dismissively and brusquely mentioned one other detail that I failed to bring to light. He reminded me that B.S. and his family had owned a multitude of brand new snowmobiles, dirt bikes and motorcycles. Remember? They were always parked in front of the house. My old man self-righteously blasted that family and said they had misplaced values, not wantonness. Really? My former elementary school empathetic and egalitarian thinking bubble shrank a bit upon hearing that smug tale from my old man and I realized that perhaps there always were two sides to a story. Misplaced values? My old-fashioned father valued a painted, well maintained, neat house and grassy lawn, and old but functional cars, rather than vice versa. I do, too, to this day. But does that way of living also give you brains?

41

Early Friendships

It was difficult to hold onto one special person that you could call a friend back then. Each class year brought in different students, transfers, as well as departing classmates. During my first formative years, rough-and-tumble P.R. was my besty, until I became his unprovoked punching bag by first grade. His Jeckyl and Hyde personality toward me was annoying and physically painful, and I broke off our weird camaraderie for good by third grade. N.K., who lived across the street and whose father was also a college professor, became a regular buddy, especially in the summertime. She was a girl, though. Nevertheless, I used to hang out on her porch on many an evening. My mom didn't worry; if I wasn't running around our street, she could usually find me jabbering with N.K. on her stoop. However, there was a plethora of similar minded comrades that always seemed to leave the school, or fail and be held back. Just when we became close, they left me in a lurch. Maybe my "Pal Picker" was broken. Then E.G. entered my life. I liked that guy, and still do. He was, and is, a good bloke. Our first encounter occurred in Mrs. M.'s third grade class. We gradually gravitated toward each other as the school year progressed. He was smart, athletic, thin, and came from a rather *strict* family at the outskirts of town. He and I had loads in common. He was even musically inclined, like me. We seemed to "get" each other, the inside jokes, the importance of book learning, the competitiveness of staying ahead of the curve in class, so to speak. Our respective parents were pushy and we both felt the pressure to excel in the classroom. Nonetheless, those unwanted but constant familial stressors seemed normal and natural to us. Our friendly union was based on mutual anxiety and performance. How sad was that? We coped as best we could, commiserated often, and played together daily on the playground at recess. We got invited to each other's requisite birthday parties, had a few play dates on weekends, and continued our bond, all the way through sixth grade, even though third grade was the last time we were physically together in the same classroom. Seventh grade saw us drift apart; we each started up with a new best friend. And so it went; life happened. Nevertheless, as our senior class yearbook attested to and personal photos bore out, we were forever buddies and never really lost touch with each other, regardless of distance. Thank you E.G. for being my friend. And I recently reconnected with N.K.; still my friend, as usual.

42

Hippie Hangman

Mrs. M. appeared as a banal, grandmotherly looking
teacher, but was in reality a gray-haired drill mistress, plain
and simple. She was tough but fair. You could smell her
cigarette breath as she made her rounds through our rows.
She smoked Camels, unfiltered. We rarely had classroom
moments of "fun" unless she officially sanctioned it. Well,
the morning show-and-tell sessions were sort of amusing
and sometimes embarrassing but otherwise, free time was a
scarce commodity in her regimented class. So on a hot
spring Friday afternoon, Mrs. M., in her usual gravelly
"Lauren Bacall" base voice, suddenly told us to put away
our reading books and pick a partner for some "craziness,"
as she bluntly put it. What was going on? I turned
quickly, looked over my shoulder and picked J.N. as my
partner. He already had the makings of a sports jock, was
not very book smart, but had a sense of humor and was a
good guy. I had known him since kindergarten. He was
Okay in my book! Plus, he actually enjoyed doing
classroom projects with me; he always got an easy A. My
best friend back then, E.G., sat across the room from me.
He also selected someone next to him. Oh, well. We had

all selected our partners and were ready. Ready for what? To dance, perhaps? NO, we were going to play Hangman on the blackboard in pairs. The duo that lasted the longest would get the prize of eating first from the cookie tray during milk and cookie time. Leave it to Mrs. M. to connect learning to fun. Darn her! Anyhow, each team in turn took to the board and tried to baffle and perplex the rest of the class. Mrs. M. had a stopwatch to time the twosomes. She wheezed that so far nobody had lasted for more than two minutes. Anyway, we students were all laughing, teasing each other and being rather boisterous. Then it was our turn. We were last. I had a word in mind and whispered it to J.N. He smiled slyly as he drew the six lines on the board and underscored the three vowel places. We mistakenly called on a smarty-pants girl who instantly got the first vowel right. Then that smart-aleck best friend of mine got the second vowel right. Holy shit, thirty seconds into our round, and we thought we had a great word! But then failure ensued. Letters and final answers were thrown at us wrongly, much to our amusement. Mrs. M. smiled and told the class that we were at four minutes and counting. Finally, at the five-minute mark, someone just plain shouted out the word: Hippie. People in the class were stunned at the word and were annoyed that we had stymied them for so long. Then slowly we watched as puzzled faces turned to admiration at our wordy effort. This was 1968, the Vietnam War and antiwar hippie movement were mutually raging and were on a collision course in the near future. You HAD to have heard of that word by third grade! My family ritualistically watched the *CBS Evening News* with Walter Cronkite, even HE had used it on occasion, in derision of course. Anyway, a beaming J.N. and I sat down and were congratulated by Mrs. M. We had won and were allowed to select the first cookies on the tray. A boy from HERE now and a boy from the neighboring hamlet of Delancey had stumped the audience with an audacious word for our elementary school times. We loved it, as did elderly Mrs. M., and she was no beatnik at heart. Or, was she?

43

The English Trailer

After the elementary school building was completed in early '62, the people of our village somehow managed to get busy, causing a minor population micro burst in the mid-sixties. And the hometown junior college also grew rapidly by hiring right and left, which contributed to the sudden influx of young professional couples, with their offspring in tow (my sister and I, for instance). The elementary school was completed with no room for expansion to accommodate the burgeoning children. What had happened? Poor planning by the school board, no birth control in town, good deer hunting with plenty of venison available for the local poor people to reproduce without hunger? Originally, there were three rooms for each grade but now four were urgently needed, at least for the second and third grades. So third grade, the last grade in the swanky but small elementary school, became the sacrificial lamb. It gave up one of its classrooms to a lower grade but received two, brand new, large, gutted out trailers that were structurally grafted onto the school, behind the parking lot, near the playground. Third grade officially had four rooms now, jam-packed with approximately 25 to 30 students apiece. A new teacher was hired for the upcoming year and we were all set to learn some serious stuff. I was in a traditional classroom but was selected to take High English from the beautiful and newly minted and hired Mrs. R., who also doubled as a third grade instructress. We did not have an accelerated math program back then, just "new math." You know, the one that kept changing yearly to make us smarter than those Soviets; the one that my dad ridiculed and called a waste of time. That math, remember? Anyhow, twice weekly, ten or so bright students from each third grade class would trudge off to Mrs. R.'s derelict trailer as her own ten would stay and the rest leave for "basic" English in my room. Forty or more kids would be packed in that rectangular dump like sardines, some standing, some sitting on the floor. The two side-by-side trailers may have been advertised as new, but in reality were chilly and drafty in the wintertime, and hot and damp in the spring and fall. The one we were in was frequently COLD and WET whenever it rained. And I'm not talking about a euphemism for beer! Mrs. R. kept up a brave front and never condemned her room. As we solemnly and silently stalked in, an obviously beleaguered Mrs. R. would begin her lecture. It was a tough slog for her. Sometimes I could not read my own writing because my lap wasn't a good surface to write on! Her trailer had tiny windows, horrible heating, fluky air conditioning, poor lighting, and the bathrooms were down the hall, to the left, next to the cafeteria. However, nobody complained. We were out to land a man on the moon someday soon and had to endure such trivial hardships in the process. I don't know how many parents today would vouch for such inferior accommodations for their "special children," or willingly pay school taxes for that. Mrs. R. was pretty, a real peach and an excellent English teacher. I had no regrets going to her class, in fact, it was mostly fun. It prepared me greatly for upcoming courses and classes. I'm not sure if those trailers are currently in use because I heard that the village population of children continued to nosedive for years after I graduated. Maybe they have been reconditioned and stuffed with rent paying adult tenants; what they were originally manufactured for in the first place.

44

Another Failing

And I thought third grade was going smoothly. Ha, ha. Wrong. Gradewise, I was killing it. I was in advanced English, math was making sense to me, and science was fast becoming my "bag." I probably knew as much about tadpoles, insects, planets, mushrooms, etc., as did my teacher, old Mrs. M. She knew it and I knew it. In other words, third grade was a breeze for me, until that dreaded, mandatory hearing/vision examination in the nurse's station, which was foisted annually on we young ones. My hearing was deemed excellent, my vision, deteriorating. At least that's what I heard the nurse tell me after I flunked the eye test. However, she added that glasses would correct my obvious nearsightedness and there was no need for worry. I would be as good as new after visiting an optometrist. Sadly I shuffled back to my class, dejected and afraid to go home with the nurse's note in my bookbag. I knew that upon reading it my dad would blow up and go nuts, and I was not disappointed. After re-reading that note after dinner, pop exploded again, blaming my mom (she is very nearsighted) and me for yet another failure. I didn't know he kept a record of my shortcomings. I felt distraught and defective, but not surprised at what went down. He was *perfect*: a handsome, athletic specimen of a man with excellent hearing, vision, balance, the works. And a high I.Q. to match. I was only eight and already behind the eight ball, dammit. And I had astigmatism, as well! After calming down and after a few weeks' time, father (he wasn't completely heartless) personally escorted me to a recommended optometrist (who became MY dental patient 40 years later) in a neighboring city and I reluctantly received my first pair of specs. Sure, I could finally see the small lettering on the blackboard but I would take them on and off as needed in school, and never wore them around the house. My best friend E.G. also procured his first set of glasses around that same time and had reservations about their full-time usage, too. But I protected those eyepieces, never got a scratch on them and never wore them in gym or when on the playground. Of course I needed periodic updates in the prescription. By sixth grade I was still sporadically wearing them, when needed. I began using them full time by eighth grade, however, because I literally had to. My distance vision had worsened to the point of necessary daily wear. I don't know why I held out for so long, probably because of the "hurt" I imagined I was causing my dad. No one in school teased me or called me names due to my diminished eyesight. Lots of kids were adorned with glasses by eighth grade, including me. I retired my coke bottle thick glasses for good in 2004, after receiving corrective Lasik surgery on both eyes at once. I need to wear "readers" for close vision now but gone were those grotesque, wire-rimmed reminders of my vision challenged youth. Good riddance. Am I now *perfect* like my old man once was? Hardly. But neither was he.

45

Clinton Street Hopscotch

I think we were wearing out the Arbuckles' carpeting, both downstairs and on the staircase leading up to our rental apartment. Although all parties still got along, I felt as if the house was suddenly full of people, all the time, and loud, too. I used to tiptoe down on Saturday mornings, sit on Mr. Arbuckle's lap, eat his candy, and watch Yogi Bear with him. He was in his late seventies and I was five at the time. We were buds. Maybe my new baby sister suddenly contributed to the overly energetic home I now lived in. Mrs. I. Arbuckle said nothing. However, the dynamics of the household had changed. It was time to move out and on, to give the owners some peace of mind, and peace and quiet for a change. We simply needed a bigger place. The Arbuckles did not object. Meanwhile my family and I had been growing into our new surroundings just fine. My father had purchased a brand new ($4,700) green-colored, Oldsmobile F-85 station wagon in 1965, was eyeing a property to purchase for a future home of our own, and my mom was busy making friends all over town. And my father was still in love with Mr. Arbuckle's late model, pristine and rarely used, tan-colored Cadillac Sedan

DeVille. Mr. A. jokingly promised my pop first dibs on the Cadi when it came time for him to buy another one. We already had a vehicle, but not a Cadillac! The initial local animosity toward us was dissipating and we were eagerly anticipating good rental news in the weeks ahead. Mom was ecstatically conversing with neighbors and showing off my sis to all comers. Our needs were broadcast by sympathetic and friendly gossipmongers and within months Mrs. Young came to our rescue. It was the good news we were waiting for. She had heard from a close friend of a friend that some "good" folks needed a place to live. She connected with my mom and a few months later we were moving in, again. It was summer, so I could help out. As pop was done with college he helped also. And then my Grandpa Pete arrived in his gray-colored, early '50s Oldsmobile, which was soon junked. He had retired from J.H. Williams and Co. (a tool and die manufacturer), and sold his house in western N.Y. He was going to live with us now! Great, just great. Well, there went my mother's few years of joy, and her sanity. I could tell she wasn't happy with the new situation but she sucked it up; he was my father's father, and family. What could she do? The move was thirty houses up from our present domicile, on the same side of the very wide street, although behind the main house facing Clinton Street. It was a legit house, but a puny one. Widowed Mrs. Young lived in the big house up front and rented out the small one in the backyard to us. I was overjoyed; finally, a real house to live in, again. It was basically a tiny Cape Cod-type, three-bedroom cottage and I had to share a cramped bedroom with my sister. Oh, well. My dad got busy securing funds and bought a crumbling former mansion not far away. He had visions and blueprints to build a proper house but a year later old Mrs. Y. approached him and asked if we could swap houses. What? She knew we were constricted and she was all alone, save for her ill-tempered dachshund named King. My dad agreed, and the rent stayed the same, $100 per month. How could you go wrong? A huge Victorian, curbside, elegant residence instead of slave's quarters. So, we moved out and in again, thirty feet away this time. The mailman's head was spinning with the address changes but all was good. Dad, grandpa and I had begun building our new home by now. Meanwhile, my sister had her own bedroom and my mom could finally invite friends over without being embarrassed by our previous living conditions. Things were looking up, or were they? Our new house fabrication was proceeding slowly, money was tight, and mom and grandpa were constantly bickering, etc. The ocean looked calm with nary a ripple, but the undercurrent was a riptide ready to suck you out to sea. I could feel the tension in our rental homes and found solace in all things buggy and amphibious. This interest of mine had slowly materialized while we still lived in the little house out back but really got going by third grade, when I was eight. It was an escape for me, to dwell on something else besides my slowly deteriorating household. Although appreciated for his meager funds, can-do spirit and helpfulness, grandfather had upset our close-knit applecart and mom was quick to point it out. But it was a double-edged sword. Our new house, being built on a shoestring budget and consisting of three workmen – dad, his dad and me – made him vitally necessary, but his old-country and chauvinistic ways drove my "modern" mom bananas and they frequently butted heads. Who was now the top dog of the family, my gruff dad or my domineering, know-it-all and workaholic grandpa? Suffice it to say that moving into our brand-new dwelling the following year would be anticlimactic for my stoic mom. To add to her familial misery in the present, however, she had heard through the village grapevine that old Mr. Arbuckle had passed away and his gorgeous and spotless Cadi had passed into the hands of a "long lost niece" who suddenly surfaced at the reading of his will. Mother consoled the widow Arbuckle and my dad mourned both losses. And grandpa? He was busy working on something, as usual.

46

The Field Trip

Oh boy, our first officially sanctioned school field trip on a bus. The entire third grade boarded four school buses and we took off. Each student was obligated to bring some cash, coins, and a homemade bagged lunch with her/his name on it. It wasn't a surprise outing, we knew about our destination well in advance. Some of my buddies, including E.G., had already been there before. I had not and looked forward to "walking among the animals." Having already been somewhat of a zoo veteran from my preschool days, I kind of knew what to expect. Our yellow-colored caravan headed south into the belly of the Catskill Mountains, to the famed Catskill Game Farm. It was supposedly filled with exotic, domestic, and tame animals for human entertainment. Tame? Before arriving, our teacher, old Mrs. M., stood up and flatly told us that the park fees were already paid for and we were free to wander about, but had to behave and then meet for lunch in the parking lot picnic area. There were no chaperones on board our bus, just Mrs. M. I don't think anyone quite heard her stern mini-lecture, for when the door opened we scattered like flies into the bowels of the animal kingdom.

No one looked back for a second. My friends and I quickly ran into the midst of a large crowd of people feeding fiber wafers to very tame but mildly aggressive white-tailed deer; the same timid kind that my old man hunted. Bambi! For a few nickels you could purchase a small bag of "specialty" treats and have the deer eat right out of one hand, while petting them with the other. No one worried about contracting ticks or Lyme disease back then. What a chaotic scene it was. Deer and humans mixed like oil and water, but both parties loved it! Next we moved onto the rides, bumper cars and Ferris wheel, then the baby animal petting section, and then the suckling area. A few nickels bought you a baby's milk bottle to feed to the friendly piglets and goats. They always seemed thirsty. Suddenly we heard the noon horn blow and had to abandon our helter-skelter pace and raced for lunch. Our labeled lunch bags of goodies were already laid out for us with the park providing sodas and cups of water. In between gulps of drink and mouthfuls of food, my frenzied friends and I plotted our afternoon capers. More running, more laughing and sightseeing seemed to be on the agenda for rambunctious eight-year-old boys. I don't know what the girls were up to and didn't care. We spent some of our dough on ice cream and candy, in between giraffe gazing and hippo watching. Ah, the gift shop. After witnessing that infamous 100-year-old-plus male tortoise go at it quite noisily and awkwardly with a female of his species, we gingerly stepped into a young lad's fantasy world. Tons of knickknacks, knockoffs, books, toys, and candies lined the overflowing shelves in that small store. However, being very appreciative of the experience and the moola my parents had given me for a day of unsupervised fun, I sought out a special present, just for them. It sounds rather nerdy and *nebbishy* but I didn't care what others thought of me at that moment. Rather than buy wooden bows, fake arrows, and bamboo spears with rubber tips on them, like all my sweaty pals did, I spied two small, plastic deer replicas, an antlered male and a doe, and paid for them. Toward evening, wired third grade ragamuffins piled onto the buses, full of sugar fueled obnoxious boys and rolled home. I think a flustered Mrs. M. wished she could have had a few drags on a Camel to calm her frayed nerves as the "Indians" danced all about her, waving their faux spears and rubber knives in the air. Remember, there were no seat belts on school buses back then to keep students buckled down. I clutched my "deer" in my hands and laughed at the spirited hooliganism surrounding me. My folks met me in the school parking lot as darkness fell, along with the other waiting parents. It had been a blast of a day. Mom was tearfully surprised by my store-bought token of gratitude and thanked me profusely. To be honest, I was surprised at her outward emotionality. They were cheap, made in Japan, miniaturized plastic, white-tailed deer reproductions. But you know, mother kept them prominently displayed on her bedroom dresser for decades. You never know how an act of kindness will touch someone, no matter how seemingly insignificant. I sometimes wonder how soon all those spears that my male classmates had bought got chucked into garbage cans after that trip?

47

Good Eggs

What an all-American intact nuclear family! And what
role models they were for me. I'm not kidding. Altruistic,
good-natured and hardworking, all rolled into one bunch
of people. A rarity to be sure but this ensemble had it all,
in spades. They maintained an immaculate green-and-
white-hued house on the corner of Clinton and Cross
streets. Everyone in the village knew them; even MY
family knew them, on a first-name basis, no less. There
was a father, a mother, two sons and a daughter. The
offspring were much older than I, however. The whole
clan worked in landscaping and law enforcement at the
time – "taking care" of the townspeople. In addition to the
various odd jobs he did, the father was in fact employed
full time as a college dormitory custodian. That would
explain his well attended and humongous, annual, end of
summer garage sale, mainly featuring the forgotten and
unwanted possessions of recently departed students. Hey,
cash-and-carry. A dime here, a dime there, you know. It's
all income. And many was the time when D.C., the
younger brother, would yell to me as I darted about
backyards, and asked me if I desired a ride on his lawn

tractor whilst cutting a neighbor's yard. He made easy money during the summers coifing the grass of the many widows on our street. With a grin, he would plop me down on his strong legs, *give me the wheel*, and step on it. I received free rides and learned how to steer a tractor. We whizzed back and forth for a while, laughing and talking loudly above the tractor's roar. After a while, I would jump off, wave a thank-you and resume my animal searches. He didn't have to do what he did, and with such enthusiasm and friendliness. I liked him a lot. There was a knock on my front door one evening that summer. My mom said it was for me. Really? Who? There stood Mr. C., with his tree-cutting crew surrounding him, as he reverently and gingerly handed me a large glass jar with a huge cecropia moth larva inside, clinging to a branch. Mr. C. beamed with delight, his crewmen were clueless, but I was enthralled and thanked him profusely. He told me he had spied it while trimming branches at the college and knew I would enjoy having that kind of caterpillar. He had heard of my "buggy" reputation and brought it over at the end of his workday. What a guy. He didn't have to do that, you know. His wife once told my mother that I should come over at night sometime and check out Mr. C.'s hobby. MY pop's indoor hobbies were horology (watch repair) and gunsmithing. I wondered what his could be? I walked over one late evening, was instantly invited in and went down to his finished cellar. He had an extensive model train setup that was professional grade. I was allowed to watch only, and I did, with my pie-hole open the entire time. He ran the trains, the miniature crossing gates, the loading and unloading platforms, etc. It was incredibly realistic looking. I thought about my Christmas train that ran in a circle under our tree. How pitiful. I went over to his house many times to observe the "running of the trains." I believe he greatly missed having a young boy in his house again; his sons were grown and on their own. But I never seized upon his unique pastime and he knew I wouldn't. Regardless, I think I was fun company for him anyway. My mom would often positively mention the C…. family in conversation. Even my suspicious and doubting pop and Grandpa Pete had to agree that some natives were indeed friendly with no ulterior motives. They were good neighbors and good eggs.

48

Building Our Dream Home

In the very early spring, before the spring peepers could peep or the Canada geese fly overhead, my Grandpa P. was already planning a vegetable garden. Now that he was retired and lived full time with us, he had nothing else to do. Having been a successful commercial farmer in Estonia in his youth, he knew his way around soil, vegetables and large farm animals. As the snow started melting, he began digging, plowing, and seeding on our new property. I remember him walking back to our Clinton Street rental house in disgust one afternoon complaining that the soil was full of sharp rocks and "purple" shaded. In Estonia the dirt was black and fertile; here, he said, "it would be a crapshoot." He was bitterly disappointed because he so looked forward to growing something again. All those years spent in a large, industrialized, city in western New York after immigrating had deprived him of his core passion. Now this "ugly" and "sickly" soil, as he put it, depressed him greatly. "I can't grow anything in this shitty mud," he would exclaim in Estonian. We hadn't even started to construct our house in earnest and he was already belly-aching about the wrong colored earth. But he did plant a few rows of this and that in his "test" garden. Well, by the time we restarted our house building a few weeks later, guess what happened? Yes, plants COULD grow amid angular rocks and in a weird colored environment. He was beyond pleased. How could this be, he asked us? He quickly scouted our new neighbors; their gardens were also growing magnificently. So he shut up, picked up the stones in his way and grew a tremendous, although tiny, garden, that first experimental year. My father had the cellar of the house "blocked" and the concrete poured for the basement floor. Because it was basically a two-man construction crew, he and my grandpa, things were not proceeding quickly. So instead of working on the house, they constructed the detached, two--car garage building first. Nosy neighbors did not know about our change of plan. Townspeople purposely drove by to "inspect" our premises as grist for the local gossip mill. But they were not privy to our plans. Anyway, by the fall of 1968, the garage was completed but instead of garage doors, old junkyard-found windows were temporarily placed to keep out the upcoming wind and snow. Well, word spread quickly. "Those 'Russkies' are poor morons," was the word on the street and what I had heard in my fourth grade class that autumn. People believed that that was going to be our hovel of a house, with old windows and no smokestacks, no ventilation, no fireplace, and left unpainted. Folks gravely shook their heads while driving by. Mr. B., a kind and sympathetic neighbor, even volunteered some old windows he had put away in storage. My father ignored all insults and snide remarks as he closed up the project for another winter. We would continue and finish in 1969. And, hopefully, move in as well.

49

Off the Deep End

All the adult members in my immediate family knew how to swim. Well, Ma did the sidestroke and doggy-paddle, but she could float like a champ. And my sister was much too young to master the drink. However, I was of age and had to learn. I was already a frequent pool visitor and now had the free opportunity to be taught the correct strokes and to stop the futile flailing and splashing about as I normally did in the shallow end. The outdoor village pool resided across the road from the high school, in its own enclosed fencing, with an unlit and rank wooden changing house behind it, and toilets underneath. Mom would walk my sister and me up the steep street at least once weekly during the summer months and watch us splash around. She would sometimes immerse herself in the kiddy pool with my sister while I braved the big pool, well, just the three-foot area. But now it was time for me to discover swimming for real, no more fooling around. School was over for the year and I excitedly welcomed the chance to become a "real" swimmer like my dad. I wanted to swim like the big kids, maybe even join the swim team someday. It was going to be fantastic, as I projected. Well, it wasn't, at least not at first. The unheated pool, the foggy, early morning frosty temperatures, and the constantly barking instructors all conspired to make those daily jaunts a pain in the neck. Is that what I signed up for? To be heckled while getting numb in ice water? There was a lot of standing around in freezing liquid, shivering, while listening and watching the poolside teachers frantically waving their arms and legs, trying to teach a bunch of frozen dainties the rudiments of the sport. However, none of them ever jumped in to join us for hands-on training. They weren't stupid. But as the summer progressed, so did I. I became better rather quickly, used kickboards, learned proper breathing techniques, and began to dive into the deep end without fear. Water was now my friend. I could tread water, swim laps and do the "crawl," as it was called years ago. On the rare occasions when neither parent could walk or drive me over, our kind-hearted neighbor, Mr. M., would do us a favor and give me a lift. I loved riding in his new car, a burgundy, four-door Buick Skylark. It was the latest in a lineup of new Buicks that he had owned. He hardly drove it anywhere but would trade it in like clockwork, in two years time, to keep things fresh, as he put it. I don't believe I ever saw him tinkering with it. Unlike my pop, who often would be elbow-deep under the hood of his '65 Olds on many weekends while Mr. M.

smiled and waved from next door. He was a recently retired former appliance store owner in town, had no children and kind of "adopted" me as the grandson he never had. His wife would often invite me over for a drink of birch beer soda if she saw me poking around their garden looking for caterpillars and butterflies. They were kind people. However, I never did join the swim team; tennis became my sport and I decided I couldn't do both at once. Anyhow, I was now a decent swimmer and easily held my own with my friends in the succeeding summers. And the deep end no longer fazed me. My wife grew up swimming in a murky and frigid Adirondack lake; I shuddered and paddled furiously in a thermally challenged outdoor pool. But our children had a different experience. Utilizing heated indoor pools, paid coaches, superbly supervised team practices, and with excellent training, both became accomplished and locally decorated swimmers; especially my son. And both kept the family's *bathing* traditions alive and well.

50

The Band Played On

The summer succeeding third grade was chock-full of life for me. Kind of like the Chocks chewable vitamins we all crunched up at the time. I chased and caught critters, interacted with my benevolent mentor Dr. R., avoided my paternal grandfather whenever possible, and marched along with the local community band on Mondays and Wednesdays. What? Yes, our dinky village boasted a full-fledged and fully instrumented community band, replete with female twirlers, color guard with pointed sticks, and with the appropriate felt banners on display. Composed of current high schoolers, and supplemented by former graduates and older players, it was a quixotic but formidable assemblage on those two weekday nights, stomping and practicing as a unit up and down Clinton Street. It was an annual event on my street. Lots of folks fondly awaited its first appearance in late June, after school let out. But why Clinton Street? Because it was the widest, least busy, and most evenly paved roadway in town. The majority of the people lining the street, including my younger sister and I, greatly enjoyed the free sounds and sights of the live biweekly performances and would relax in lawn chairs while watching the mini parade go back and forth. Mr. S., the chunky and sweaty band leader, would frequently halt the slow-moving stampede to correct the cadence, steps and musicianship of the participants. He could be a demanding boss, which resulted in notes emanating from flutes, French horns and trombones that were ALWAYS on cue. He would also direct traffic should an automobile owner wish to pull into her/his driveway. Mrs. R., the other necessary volunteer, controlled the baton twirlers and color guard routines. As amateurs, the band members performed well together. My sister and I, when not peddling five cent lemonade cups from a makeshift stand in front of our rental house, would dutifully strut along the sidewalk to the beat of songs such as *Georgy Girl* and *Downtown*. The rehearsals usually lasted a few sweltering hours, weather permitting. Then the asphalt-hardened musicians would quickly pack up their instruments and vanish. They performed at officially sanctioned town functions such as the Fourth of July and Labor Day parades as well as for Friday night festivities every August, on the Village Square. The yearly bands were always good, by my limited standards, and gave the normally placid Clinton Street a kick, twice a week, during the hot summer months. No one complained about the "noise." And even when we had moved away from Clinton

Street and into our new house, I could still clearly hear the blaring trumpets, the boom of the bass drum and oboe squeaks, from my front yard; it was village living at its best.

Take a break!

FOURTH GRADE

51

Movin' On Up, and Down

Finally, we would be free of that dang elementary school and start *learnin'* where the big kids were jailed. Finally! The relatively new elementary school was set on a bluff, actually on a side of a large hill, above the high school and sports fields. We little tykes had a grand view of the college across the valley and the large, looming warehouse of our future education down below. The high school's gigantic and majestic tower had four clocks mounted near the top, just underneath the weathervane. You could never be late if you just looked up a bit, from any direction. There was a pedestrian connection with intermittent steps and handrails all the way up from the high school to our elementary building's doorstep. Back then this walkway was used twice daily because many of us walked to school, and home again, in those "safe" times. No one worried about getting abducted and molested during those halcyon and naïve days. Anyway our legs and lungs were probably strengthened by our forced daily marches down one mountain and up the next, so to speak. Sure, sometimes we took the bus to school, on rainy days for instance and on snowy, wintry mornings as well. But for the most part, it was leg power that got us to class and back home. Most parents didn't drive us to class or pick us up after school either. A lot of mothers didn't drive and fathers were at work, with the only family car. This was the late '60s, remember? Anyhow, fourth grade started and during recess I wistfully remember looking up those flights of stairs to view our former torture chamber. No more rusty and banged up bannisters to clutch and concrete steps to count. We were big shots now. We got off the bus in front of the main building with the older students. We had moved up in our education and down the hill. Was it metaphorically and prophetically all downhill from here on in? Probably. Of course, once a year we had an emergency bus drill where all the buses, with all the children on board, would purposely stop at the elementary school and discharge us from the rear door emergency exit. We then had to walk down the steep and sporadically staired incline to the main school. It always brought back a sense of melancholy juxtaposed with achievement. Even as a senior I was still made to walk down those steps of yesteryear, at least yearly. Was I a sentimental sap or just plain tired of walking so much? Perhaps both. But I will tell you that my calves are still shapely after all these years.

52

That Nerve-Wracking Stank

I don't know about you but the first day of school always made me nervous. You know, agitated. Fear of the unknown you might say. Although I was not a transfer student and attended the same educational settings with the same group of cohorts, I still felt anxious, especially during every year's initial break-in week. Fourth grade was in the big building, the high school, where the big kids were, where the halls were barely lit up by incandescent lamps and where the floors in each classroom were hardwood oak with a slick polyurethane finish. Unlike the "modern" elementary structure (K-3), the high school was a bit behind the times and had that 1930's motif going strong (it was built in 1939). We youngsters were used to bright fluorescent lighting and polished linoleum flooring as in our previous K-3 building. However, our elementary school wing (4-6 grades) in the high school was also very high-ceilinged, scantily lit, and had wood flooring. Just before school started each autumn, the custodians would relacquer the planking with a coating of polyurethane to give it that hard, impervious, sheenful finish, although with a stench to match. The gloss was impressive but the stank, horrid. Dammit, I began to associate the first day of school with that rueful stink. Olfactory effects are a bitch. And every first day of school thereafter through my senior year reminded me of my anxiety-laden first week of fourth grade. That primordial angst never left me. Even now, whenever I inhale polyurethane vapors, I tense up. Attending my children's "back to school" nights brought back "painful" recollections for me, much to the amusement of my wife and kids. Their respective elementary school classrooms had that same malodor in the air. Some things you just can't shake, or outgrow.

53

The Big House

We had made the journey from the puny elementary
school to the Big House, the main high school building,
although grades 4-6 had their own first floor wing,
complete with a kiddy library room. I made it past the
polyurethane stench, past the main office, found the right
room number and stumbled in. Standing inside the
doorway was a freshly minted teacher, Mrs. L. She was
gorgeous: an olive-skinned complexion, a killer body, a
short black hairdo, and with a smile a mile wide. Now
THAT was the way to welcome nervous students to a new
environment on the first day of fourth grade. Although no
longer in the ultramodern (by early sixties standards)
elementary school anymore, nevertheless we were still
considered grammar school grunts, hence our own hallway,
where older students were discouraged to trespass without
good reason. I had been in the high school before,
spectating afterschool performances and plays in the
old-fashioned auditorium and dated gymnasium. The high
school was a strange and cold place, one that readily
echoed even the slightest sounds. Tall ceilings with paltry
incandescent lighting, hard marble floors in the hallways,

varnished oak flooring in the classrooms, tall windows, bland beige tiling on the sides of the hallways and lockers as far as the eye could see. I assumed the second floor was the same. It was. The rooms' doors were wooden with a window in each. But to be fair, it was built in 1939; however, it was hard to find any new updates to that edition. The red brick outside was grandiose, with granite columns and wide stone steps at the entrance. It was a cupola and clock tower bestowed school worthy of a postcard picture. It was grand looking and we little fourth grade dweebs felt proud to be there, at least I did. Anyhow, after introductions and alphabetical seating behind scribbled on wooden desks attached to hard wooden seats in rows, the lovely Mrs. L. began her *teacher's shtick*. You know, the usual outline of what was expected of us; the rules, regulations, special topics covered during the school year, blah, blah, blah. I was too busy watching her every movement to have heard all the details. I wasn't the only one. As I scanned the room, the usually noisy boys were quiet, with eyes on Mrs. L. It reminds me of that 1984 Van Halen music video *Hot for Teacher*. Our first major topic was going to be nutrition, she announced. In addition to the requisite short bursts of other daily subjects, such as English and math, we were required to discuss, compile and write down a week's worth of breakfast foods that we ate each morning. No problem. I often wondered why that particular topic was chosen, and why so early in the year? Even then I suspected that some of our rural poorer students were getting less to eat than their dairy cows and had inadequate human caloric intakes. My suspicions were born out when we were forced to divulge our written notes outloud the following week. Each student in every row spoke up about her/his morning food intake while Mrs. L. nodded and took careful notes. It became painfully apparent that a glass of water and half a donut were considered subpar, as some embarrassed students found out. They could have lied and made up tasty sounding foodstuffs instead but obviously they did not. Mrs. L. had no comments. But then she offered a challenge. The row that had the best weekly breakfasts would win a prize of her choosing. Well, that got the whole class motivated to make a.m. dining better. Naturally, my row won. We each received a coupon for a free book from the upcoming "Library Day." However, being an observant student, there were two takeaways from that first topic: The notes Mrs. L. jotted down were probably names of at-risk students that most likely appeared malnourished. Sure enough, the newly started, early morning, free breakfast program in the main cafeteria had new fourth graders in it. I saw some of my classmates exiting that food hall just as I was going to class. It was a great idea and no one was embarrassed by it. And one more thing. I called the liquid that was excreted by female cows – milk. Most of my "farm bred" class brethren pronounced it – *malk*. Was it rural slang or what? No one corrected ME when I said I had two pieces of toast, a hard-boiled egg and a glass of MILK for breakfast. But boy did I ever want to rectify some of my row mates and others that posed that they had consumed farina, bacon and MALK. I squirmed uncomfortably in my seat but resisted. Mrs. L. caught my annoyed facial expressions and chuckled many times to herself while shushing me with a finger to her lips. I think we were both in on the same joke. I loved her.

54

Bathroom in the Basement?

My remaining original classmates and I had successfully navigated third grade, passed into fourth, moved down to the main high school building and were all set when school commenced that fall day. But where do we urinate and lay our bricks? In the elementary school, each classroom had a tiny but fully functional defecation unit, with a door on it, tucked away near the entrance, next to the coat rack. I didn't see such a space in our large, square, fourth grade classroom. Now what? Well, before we were even seated, Mrs. L., a brand new, beautiful and enthusiastic teacher, immediately told all of us yakking and disorderly greenhorns that if we had to "go," we could walk down the hall to the basement and then to return quickly. This would be our only chance before class began. After that we would all go as a group during scheduled bathroom breaks. I was listening intently but the word basement confused me. Was the bathroom really in the basement of the school? Were there directions on how to locate it? Wasn't it dingy and stinky down there, like all cellars are? All these thoughts raced through my head at once. I decided to hold it. I didn't want to get lost on the first day of school! Well, at ten o'clock, Mrs. L. told us all to line up in front of the door and listen to her directions; our first bathroom break was commencing. We were expected to behave when outside our class. Boys and girls marched silently down the hallway in two sex-separated lines. We were the only students in the hall. I assumed the other elementary grades and individual classes had their own break times. Then Mrs. L. quietly whispered HALT. Obediently, we stopped and looked around. There were two doors marked *Men's* and *Women's*, on opposite sides of the hallway. There they were, the bathrooms, on the first floor, just down the hall from our room. The few daredevil souls that had already visited the "can" had knowing and smug looks on their faces. I was bug-eyed. We were allowed entry to do our business, in groups of four, and lined back up upon exit. On the return trek to our room, I sheepishly asked Mrs. L. why the word "basement" was used. She laughingly explained that the word "bathroom" sounded gross and "basement" was the politically correct word used at our esteemed school. Now, I don't know if all high schools used that same word as a euphemism for the shitter, or just our school. What if the colloquial word had been something else? Would we neophytes be going to the "pizzeria" or "gas station?" It's funny that even as high school seniors I remember hearing the word "basement" whenever one of my peeps had to pee. Even I used that word. It's interesting what you get used to as being the norm. And, what's normal?

55

First Crush

I had casually dabbled in the opposite sex since preschool; that was the heterosexual male standard back then. Nothing lascivious at that age, just a cursory curiosity in girls, especially the pretty ones. Although there were the obligatory late bloomers in our grade, most of the future hot babes showed potential early on, even while in elementary school. They knew it and we boys knew it, at least at some prepubescent level. Fortunately, hormones did not kick in and *rule* us until many years later. We interacted on the playground, but boys usually played with boys, girls with girls. We even had sexually separate gym classes starting in first grade. However, they were part of our species and sat next to us; our mothers were girls! Anyway, I met this certain attractive *yellow flower* in my kindergarten class but then she kind of disappeared from my life. Although I caught sporadic glimpses of her at recess and lunch, she had different teachers for first, second and third grades. Now in fourth grade, there she sat, a few seats ahead of me, and she appeared more lovely than ever. I felt differently around her now. I hobnobbed with other females daily but she was special. She gave me butterflies in my stomach, my heart thumped in her presence. I had the "fever" but it wasn't yet spring. She was pleasant to me but did not reciprocate the feelings I had for her. Or maybe I just couldn't tell? I even tried to make an inroad with her old man, our village postmaster, with no luck. I was in the antiquated town post office with my mom one day when he sauntered out of his private den. Surprisingly, I summoned up my limited courage and boldly said, "Hi, Mr. B., I like your girl." He paused, looked down at me and replied, "That's nice," and smiled at my mother with a puzzled look on his face. And that was that. The crush I had on his daughter started to fade and by years end it was over. To my knowledge she never seemed all that interested in me. She and her four sisters were beautiful blue-eyed blondes and were eye-popping candy for we horny male teenagers for years, as we slowly matured. Besides being attractive they were also intelligent and very athletic. But in those stone-age days, beauty beat out brains in our Neolithic minds. And, as pretty women they always had boyfriends! Nothing had ever materialized between S.B. and me as we both grew older and finally graduated, but I'll never forget that first crush. Maybe I should contact her and find out how she really felt about me over fifty years ago? Perhaps not.

56

Tinkertoys, LEGO and Lincoln Logs

It began as a slow accumulation but by fourth grade, I whittled down my extensive *building toys* collection to three favorites: Tinkertoys, multicolored LEGO, and Lincoln Logs. They became my stalwart and go-to toys whenever a "constructive" thought crossed my young mind, which was fairly often, especially during seasonally inclement weather. I did possess a new Erector Set, which had been bought for me years earlier, but, nonetheless, I never warmed up to it. It seemed overly complex. It was too much: all those tiny nuts and bolts and detailed instructions to follow. Many times I became motivated to use the set but quickly abandoned all hope in erecting something that resembled the enclosed diagrams. I think my faux "love" of engineering had its limits and I stuck to simple blocks and sticks. My sister's playing at the time alternated between dressing Barbie dolls and manipulating the features of Mr. Potato Head and Cooky the Cucumber, all purchased as birthday gifts at our town's Western Auto store on Main Street. Yes, we both took turns with the Etch A Sketch, too. We occupied our personal indoor time using our minds and hands. We didn't have mindless video games that only require the use of thumbs. I would build elaborate structures and supplemented the miniature buildings with many hardbound textbooks as added foundations, and even attempted some primal Rube Goldberg scenarios. You know, making a complicated maze of interacting parts for an obviously and ridiculously simple outcome. Sometimes I would design a construction site that involved books, rulers, spools and small chutes, in addition to using other readily available building materials. A marble was dropped at a suitably high starting point and then watched as it picked up speed, meandering through my mini-obstacle course, coming to an end on the floor. It was fun to alter the various routes I had set up and then see which one was the fastest for the marbles to negotiate. I sometimes compare my former childlike thoughts and actions to my childrens': My daughter eschewed dolls, played with her plastic dinosaur set and muddied herself almost daily while hunting for insects and slimy creatures. My son, born visually impaired, never sought to build anything, or sully himself in any way. His thing was sports, playing dress-up, video viewing, and, shortly thereafter, embracing computers and hand-held gaming devices. My daughter is now a scientist, an entomologist; my son, an attorney. And me? I ended up becoming a microengineer of the oral cavity: a dentist!

57

Nuclear Arms

Fourth grade was in the big building, with the tall hallways, dim lighting for we dimwits, and it was a testament to learning the old-fashioned way, the 1930's way, although it was now 1968. When we had our occasional fire drills back in the grammar school, we would dutifully file out of school, wait for the all clear, and file back in. The same went for the high school. However, the nuclear attack siren sounds for each school were distinct from one another, and with subsequently different approaches to self-preservation should an atomic bomb actually detonate near our village. In the elementary school, a series of short and shrill bursts of noise forced us students to crawl under our desks and remain in a fecal (or fetal) position until the teacher told us it was over. In the high school, a loud horn would play over the announcement system denoting the atomic drill. As per proper protocol, ALL students in the high school building would quickly run out into the hallways, silently line up and hug the nearest tile-lined wall, bore their foreheads hard into it, and put their arms over the tops of their heads and patiently wait for the principal's all clear utterance. And no talking! Any silliness would not be tolerated. This was serious business. Teachers would walk around reprimanding derelict students and correcting poor positioning of arms and legs. It was deemed important and OBVIOUSLY would have been a deterrent to the thermal blast and gobs of radiation that would occur in real life. Are you kidding me? There was no official bomb shelter at our public schools and the one my pop built as part of our house basement probably could have stopped a mortar shell but not anything larger or deadlier. I'm sure the Soviet children prepared the same way we did; two countries at the brink of nuclear holocaust all through the sixties with their citizens naively trusting that proper attention to detail during strict rehearsals would protect them. What a laugh. Thousands perished instantly in the Hiroshima blast and I don't think their arm positions mattered one iota.

58

Halloween

All Hallow's Eve was and is a favorite pseudoholiday for
my family and me. Although immigrants, my parents
quickly embraced this "strange" American custom that was
thrust upon them every October 31. As a young trickster I
never missed one, even when sick as a dog or fighting early
snowflakes and, sometimes, wintry chill. Late autumn was
always a special and magical season for me. First my
birthday, then Halloween, both in the same month! I
loved it. And my village, especially Clinton Street, fully
and safely cooperated with the hundreds of munchkins let
loose on that one night. Costumed children of all ages
scurried from lighted house to house demanding sweets
from the generous and mostly sweet purveyors of the
goods. Kids would venture forth at sundown, without any
parental supervision, flashlights, pepper spray or mace. We
would all hit the poorly lit streets en' masse like candy-
deprived vultures looking for easy treats. But the
cooperative townspeople were also eagerly awaiting us with
the same anticipatory fervor. There was no need for tricks.
Children ran across dewy, manicured lawns, up steep stairs,
and were sometimes invited into homes by curious

homeowners. No one got raped, molested or kidnapped in our town. At age four my sister was deemed ready for combat and she was chomping at the bit to get out there and snag some sugar. She emphatically told my mom and pop that she could keep up with me, so we went together that Halloween. I was newly nine and a seasoned pro at this snack begging ritual. She was a newbie but proved to be a quick study. She was dressed as a clown, and I the Batman. It was always a fight with my mom as to whether we should wear our chintzy outfits on top of our warm coats, underneath them, or without any additional layers at all. Some Octobers were warm, some were not. So, out we went, together for the first time. It was a blast, especially when meeting up with classmates that I knew well. Mini gangs would spontaneously form as we canvassed Clinton, Cross, Second and Franklin streets in ragtag groups. I knew from experience which homes gave out the largest candy bars and which ones gave "worthless" apples or bananas. I also knew which owners purposely "tricked" unknowing kids into coming inside their dwellings and tried to guess who they were before unmasking them. But sometimes even I got suckered into a home. The year my sister tagged along with me I was not only an older brother but a teacher. She nodded reverently as I explained which homes to avoid and which ones to go back to twice, or three times. It was a sacred ritual that had to be memorized! And of course we got bamboozled into entering Miss Hayes' house with a bunch of other unhappy saps. We stood there, inhaling the damp odors of her old house and sweating uncomfortably under our masks and outfits. She took her time trying to guess who we five were. We finally took off our facial facades and she beamed with delight. She had gotten all of us right. We opened our bags wide expecting special rewards but received small apples instead. What a gyp from that crusty old maid. She was a long retired local school teacher. We dupes had gotten duped by that witchy bitch for the last time, I promised my sister. We quickly left her porch in a huff and promptly threw away the red fruit in our bags. It wasn't candy, so there. And who knows how long she had been touching those MacIntosh with those disgusting and wrinkled fingers of hers? Yuck. No one ate apples on that night, no one. By nine o'clock, we were home with our paper shopping bags dumped of their contents, busily devouring and counting our stashes of savory morsels. But they had to be wrapped to be eaten. Any unwrapped or unpackaged candy was promptly tossed by mom. And any fruit, well, you know.... we had tossed it before getting home. Now came part two of the night. We left our piles of chocolates, sweet tarts and sourballs at home, jumped into our family station wagon and were quickly whisked away by our father to the elementary school gymnasium for a school sponsored party, complete with games and more delicious cakes and confections to dine on. There was no begging this time. But I did see Mrs. P. there, the old playground monitor from a few years back. She had devilishly delighted in having us play endless rounds of *Ring Around the Rosie* and *Duck, Duck, Goose* for her seemingly deranged amusement whenever we had to stay inside that very gym for recess, due to inclement weather. I had hated those silly games, and her, as well. Everyone loaded up from the trays of sugary edibles and we were home by 10 p.m. What a night. My parents raptly listened to our ghoulish adventures as we chewed and talked, and made sure to complement my sister on a job well done. Today's youthful October 31 rituals revolve around expensive costumes, sanctioned school parades with requisite photo ops, visiting the local mall before sunset, carpooling kids along streets, walking children up to doors, and carefully inspecting candy as if each piece had a pin or razorblade in it. How times have changed. But MY Norman Rockwell-type Halloweens had been blessedly different, thank goodness. I vividly remember being glad to have moved to this "unknown" village instead of still living in my old city where decent, law-abiding adults rarely ventured out at night, no matter the special occasion. And forget about the kids. I guessed correctly that a dumpy and dinky town full of dumpy dinks was not a bad place to grow up in after all. Maybe I would start to fit in better as time went along. Perhaps I should be more patient, I thought; and I was right, to a point.

59

Healthy Annuals?

Even in a rural central school with a small student population, health screenings were deemed important. Medical and dental exams were performed annually on elementary school scholars in the nurse's station, the one with the sign above the door that read Nurse's Station. Always wearing huge muumuu dresses, Mrs. M.D. was the obese and virtually catatonic high school nurse for grades 4-12. It was mandatory for we *schlubs* in grades 4-6 to visit her yearly. But any student with a medical emergency or illness excuse was obligated to see her, as necessary. Starting in fourth grade, the yearly physical consisted of a physician from town being present, as well as Mrs. M.D. Boys stood in line on the appointed day, dressed only in our tighty-whities, and stood barefoot, freezing in her cold office. No one wore boxers in those days. Well our grandfathers did, but not us! She examined our necks for mumps and then ran her meaty hands over our bodies in a search for unwanted lumps. She took our vitals in a cursory manner, wrote down her findings, and then handed us over to the doctor who put his chilly hand on our groins and made us cough. He was checking for hernias and was not a pedophile, I hope. He was not my family doctor, though. I didn't know him, no one seemed to. Oh well, we got our privates patted by him, got dressed and went back to class. If a problem was detected, Mrs. M.D. would send a note home with you. Some of my friends did indeed get a note from her but I never inquired as to what their particular medical maladies were. They all reappeared in class the next day and most graduated on time with me. The school nurse would also function as the morning person to see if you were tardy or had been sick. She carefully read the parents' handwritten excuses, would nod disapprovingly and in fantastic cursive writing methodically jot down the illness you supposedly had on an index card that had your name on it. The school had to keep accurate records to be funded by the "state." All students had to be accounted for, truant or not. If you felt unwell or needed a change of clothes during the day, her office would also oblige you. You could be excused by a teacher at will and at least go in for a lie-down due to a migraine or stomachache. If things became serious, your parents would be notified to come pick you up. There were always a few kids of all ages in the gurney room, recovering from sprains, pains and stomach problems. I was an infrequent visitor but succumbed to a few transient illnesses over the years. That's what the station was there for. Mrs. C., the usually soused and friendly school dental hygienist, was in the same office but had a separate, tiny room. Also a necessary annual evil, she would poke and prod your teeth and gums, write down her findings, and then polish your choppers with gritty prophy paste before imploring you to spit into her stained cuspidor. If you had a dental problem, such as gum disease or an obvious cavity, she would send a note home for the student's folks to deal with. X-rays were not taken by her, only a quick visual exam was done. I guess she hoped or assumed that we students were already seeing our local family dentist on a regular basis and needn't be so thorough. Most of my classmates did not. However, she never found anything dentally amiss in my mouth and I was grateful and relieved. I did visit old Dr. Smithe at least yearly and eventually needed an extraction, a stainless steel cap on a front tooth, and minor orthodontics to get me straightened out. But that occurred a few years into the future. But for fourth grade purposes, I was dentally boring and in a mixed dentition state: a few remaining baby teeth mingled with adult teeth. All good and normal for a nine-year-old.

60

Recess Trekkies

That penchant for role-playing based on a popular sci-fi TV show started in third grade and continued into fourth. "Mike" was the ringleader and played Captain Kirk, obviously. He was the same kid, that in my third grade classroom the previous year, stood up one morning and at the top of his lungs yelled, "Stop calling me G...., my name is Mike." It really wasn't, maybe it was his middle name? Anyway, he had grown tired and frustrated at being teased for having an "effeminate-sounding" given name. One day he couldn't take it any longer and thus the sudden and anguished proclamation. Mrs. M. intervened later that afternoon and made the whole class promise to call him Mike from now on, as he sat there red-faced and gritting his teeth. So we called him Mike from then on. He wasn't a bad kid, not a bully, just someone who was at the end of his wits with put-upon shame. And also we ceased ribbing him. Anyway, Mike loved the new *Star Trek* TV show and decided to emulate the characters at recess with a like-minded bunch of pseudo thespians. What started as an infantile attempt at play acting morphed into uniforms and toy phasers for the all-male participants. He and his band of playactors monopolized certain sections of the playground and used the slide and swing sets as background props. I had seen a few episodes of the TV show but was not a regular viewer. You needed to be a hard-core aficionado and diehard devotee to get a select part in his group's action drama. I would sometimes watch, puzzled at the goings-on. Even the dark-haired and serious N.Z., who played Spock, was into the act. He was a quiet and scientifically oriented contemporary of mine though not in my particular classroom. His fourth grade teacher was Mrs. F., next door. He and I seemed to have a good deal in common though we never hit it off. Although scholastically and athletically my equal, he most likely regarded me as a "smart" buffoon, and he was probably right. But who was the REAL idiot? Izzy, who did not participate in stupid charades with a would-be impresario who insisted on being called Captain during recess? Or was it N.Z., who looked down at me as the class clown, yet buzzed around the teetertotters making screeching phaser-blast sounds and who looked ridiculous in his homemade Starfleet outfit, complete with taped on ear tips? Let me tell you, all the nearby girls giggled at those nerds. The stylized playing was often marred with infighting and arguments about the correctness of the copied recent TV episode. I witnessed lots of standing around instead of *acting* because Mike did not like the way things were progressing. So much time was wasted on training inept improv actors that recess would sometimes end before a "Tricorder could accurately be read by Bones." It was all silly stuff, at least in my mind. I scoffed and laughed in their general direction whenever I passed that group of geeks. To be fair, Mike, who fancied himself a natural leader, did ask me to play sci-fi make-believe a few times, but to be the villain, not an honorable officer. I had declined on more than one occasion. I was never a fan of the show, had not watched it enough, and still called him G…. in my mind. He was not MY leader. Was I subconsciously envious that he could corral and control a whole swatch of willing fourth graders? Perhaps. Nonetheless, the playground action-adventure series ended by fifth grade. I wonder what ever happened to Mike and his overcompensating bravado? Was he still G…. at heart? Gene Roddenberry didn't seem to mind his first name. So, there!

61

Tennis!

Let me put it this way: If my father had been an ardent basketball or baseball player, I would most likely have been either dribbling or hitting a ball with a bat. Instead, he was a professor of engineering and a talented tennis coach at his college. He had been a standout player in his university days and was "forcibly" recruited to coach the fledgling tennis team at his new place of employment. He couldn't say no back in those days. At age nine, he stuck a nylon-strung, wooden Wilson Jack Kramer tennis racquet in my hand and loudly proclaimed, "You are now a tennis player, here is your weapon." The Wilson Jack Kramer model racquet was the state of the art in those days and very popular among college players. So I became a tennis player overnight and joined the family sport. And that was that. Although a formidable and former champion table tennis player and multisport athlete, my pop's love was, and is, tennis. Like father, like son; I followed suit. Although I did become a very respectable ping pong player and track athlete, the countless hours spent on court with my dad also made me a very good tennis player, by high school standards, that is. The equipment was wooden, the fuzzy balls were white, and our shorts were way too short. But I learned quickly and by my junior year was ranked first in Section IV, Class B. Sure, I had inherited his talent, developed my own big serve and an even bigger forehand, but the learning process had not been easy. Pop approached every project with perfection in mind and was a tough-ass coach. Some days I felt like quitting. That's the way it goes sometimes. And we only played for three seasons because there were no indoor courts where we lived. We played table tennis during the long upstate N.Y. winters in the late sixties and early seventies. The end results? I still play tennis regularly, indoors, too. And I have been a competitive, nationally ranked singles player in various age groups as I have grown older. And my old man? He still plays; doubles only, however. My sister, wife and daughter also play. What a wonderful lifetime sporting gift my father gave me and my family. Thanks dad.

62

Projects

Growing up hearing that word, or the singular of it, always made me weak in the knees, anxious, and mental. After moving into our new house, which was barely finished, there were the odd carpentry, plumbing and tile jobs that needed to be completed to have a finished look about the place. I was fine with that and understood the importance of those tasks, which were mostly accomplished on winter weekends when my father was home and not teaching. Grandpa Pete masterminded the work to be concluded, because he had nothing better to do all day, and always had a carefully laid out plan of execution. Pop usually agreed with him and conscripted me into those assignments as if I was just loafing around and itching to get involved. They always were astounded that I wasn't more enthusiastic about "helping" out. Their idea of me helping was watching for hours on end as a bored dolt, standing there, looking helpless and pathetic. I was supposed to be "learning" by seeing them sweat and work hard. It was considered "manly" and I should have been proud to be by their sides as a young apprentice. Gag me! Everyone knows that you learn by doing, not by observing. However, I couldn't touch anything for fear of doing something "wrongly." And God forbid if I had an excuse not to participate in the weekend's work charade. I was castigated, humiliated, and deemed worthless whenever I skipped out on the *home show*, which was often. How would I ever learn how to lay tile, or nail veneering onto two-by-fours, or fix a leak in the bathroom faucet? I was labeled a lazy loser more than twice. Once our home became more or less finished, my workaholic grandpa turned to his large garden and outdoor activities to constantly keep himself, my sister and me busy. In his mind we still lived on a farm in Estonia and *needed* to work from sunup to sundown. Never mind that he worked in a tool and die factory upon immigration for nearly two decades. Living in the country again seemed to have reawakened his farmer genes and we suffered for it. During the summers it got to the point where I had to sneak away unseen in the mornings to chase butterflies in some distant field, or literally jump on my bike and pedal off like a madman into town, or sprint at top speed to the brook for salamander salvation. If I hung around I would instantly be roped into "watching" or relegated to a supervised mundane gig. I did help out in the garden picking up endless stones that surfaced daily, and I regularly picked off Colorado potato beetles from the potato plants, etc. However, the chores were endless: changing the oil, filters and mufflers on our cars, replacing whole engines as needed, etc. As soon as one job was done, another was planned for. If he was exerting himself and I was not, the guilt trip was awful. I approached weekends with trepidation and dread. Sure, we saved a ton of money by being frugal and were "blessed" with his energy and know-how, but at what cost? I never objected to saving money or doing things the "right" way but it was the gravitas of constantly working that drove me nuts. "Eat, sleep and work" was his mantra. Even my perfectionist dad had to put his foot down on many occasions for us to go on vacations, to play tennis, ping pong, fish, or hunt, much to the judgmental disapproval of my grandfather. My mom often forcibly ferried my sister and me to the village pool for some afternoon "fun" while under duress at the home front. The projects were endless and maintenance of our home and autos took on a circuitous nature. Something constantly needed mending or attention. It was nonstop. Grandpa seemed ageless and never once behaved as a "normal" elderly man whose grandkids (my sister and me) could easily gravitate to and learn wisdom from. There was little time in his *busy* daily schedule for gentleness, frivolity, reading, pleasure, intellectual pursuits, or sports. Physical toil was his elixir of life and I deeply resented it, and him. I graduated from high school, pharmacy college and dental school as a learned doctor and hated to come home with my own family in tow because of his latent and loathing snide remarks directed at me and my children! It was a terrible feeling. My mom's parents lived far away, also in western New York State, but I liked to visit them, nonetheless. They were nonjudgmental and loved me regardless of my work ethic. I always wished my Grandpa Pete could have metamorphosed into a kind, generous and selfless human being and made time to "smell" his grandchildren, take them on educational walks, and be a reservoir for unconditional love. It never happened. The longer he lived with my family the more he soured his relationship with my mom, my dad, my sister and me. He died and the earth did not stop spinning, as he had predicted. All the unfinished work magically got rendered, the lawn was mowed, the garden planted, the oil changed and ball joints lubed. I heard that my pop downsized a little and had to spend some cash on things he couldn't fix but proved to be a talented master of ALL trades. Besides his athletic, artistic and professorial attributes, he could also do masonry, carpentry, sew, tailor clothing, precisely repair watches (he was a bona fide horologist), guns, autos, toasters, radios, etc., all by himself, and without berating my mom in the process. SHE became my dad's apprentice and accomplished coworker, as needed, and errands managed to get fulfilled. Had all those years growing up in the shadow of harsh browbeating from an overbearing and headstrong grandfather been for naught? Perhaps. His obvious addiction to hard labor was HIS deal, HIS therapy, not mine. I think I made out okay though, as did my sister, but at what psychological price? And my wife sardonically reminds me that I kept our own children "busy," sometimes making them do things against their wills. Many times that was true, but I never ever conscripted them into useless standby duty as my helpless "helpers." Nevertheless, I continually find MYSELf *work* to do, to this day. Or does *work* find me? Regardless, it's that damn DNA of Grandpa Pete's that's inside of me! I still hate that word: projects!

63

It's a Garage!

Wow. 1969 was fast approaching. Who knew that
Woodstock would "happen?" Who knew that America
would successfully put a man on the moon? And who
knew that my family and I would finally cross the
threshold into our brand new house? Well, all those things
DID happen. Toiling away sporadically all winter in the
sealed off basement of our new construction, my father and
grandfather emerged in the springtime like hibernating
woodchucks, not famished but hungry to finish that dang
dwelling and move in! As previously mentioned, neighbors
and nosy *nudniks* sympathetically but wrongly assumed
that our window-paned, separate garage was going to be
our home. Suddenly, two huge garage doors appeared on
the "house," the roofing was completed and the sides
painted. Well, the rage from some villagers just poured out
in loud, profane tones: "How dare those 'dirty Russians'
fool us? It was a garage all along, not a house. Screw
them! And that garage is bigger than some village homes!"
My pop heard the bullshit all around him and laughed.
"But if that's the garage, how large will the house be?,"
some noisy fellas exclaimed in disbelief, almost in unison.

NOW they were interested in the project again, amid much speculation and disgust. Slowly and with measured accuracy, the large rectangular first floor took shape. "It's going to be a large ranch-style," said one onlooker while cracking a cold one. My pop stayed quiet during breaks in the building process, however. I was mostly there on weekends and, besides helping out, heard most of the comments and profanities from the peanut gallery that assembled daily on the sidewalk. By now the onlookers had found out that my dad was a civil engineer/architect/ college professor and probably knew what he was doing. NOW the interested yokels wanted to see just what tricks a "pro" had up his sleeve. Palpable and vocal envy turned to angry curiosity. As the second story two-by-fours and plywood pieces fell into shape, the naysayers started up the name calling again. "A second floor? Damn them," cursed one burly man, while forcibly squeezing his empty beer can. "He's building a castle," another growled indignantly. However outraged, all stayed put to keep watching the *show*. By the summer, the house was completed. I vividly remember pounding nails into the plywood flooring that would be my bedroom. Even my sister and mom helped out on most of those warm weekends. Some of my father's architectural artistry did not come to fruition, however. Lack of funds, expediency and building complications thwarted the construction of a few flying buttresses, porches on the second floor, and a small turret. It turned out to be a large, rectangular, four-bedroom building with beige-painted clapboards and a chimney. Nothing too fancy. The landscaping was done and the grass seed broadcast by hand. The curiousity seekers had vanished making our delayed and overdue entrance rather uninspiring. As grandpa was finishing the roofing, he posited that no one was complaining anymore. Good. I was overjoyed. Our own place, my own bedroom. Yay! Our own big backyard. There were a lot of unfinished little things that were gradually worked on but we received the certificate of occupancy and were in our own new house, at last. But I had psychologically never abandoned Clinton Street, and would continue to revisit my old neighborhood on foot and by bike for years to come. Now I had two outdoor playgrounds and multiple yards to traverse as an intrepid hunter of insects and other slimy minibeasts. Plus, the untamed farm field behind our new property, which wasn't posted, held promise as a new frontier for hiking and exploration. I was happy. Just one more aside: a former inebriated *kibitzer* did get a last dig into my father, however. He confronted my old man in our driveway one day and chortled, "Good luck with the taxes on your mansion." My father froze. And to this day the driveway is stoned and unpaved, for fear of the local taxman raising the assessment any more than it already is. Yes, the paranoia is still there, but it may be justified!

64

The Blind Man

My own son was born severely visually impaired. Although finishing as the valedictorian of his prep school class, earning an Ivy League bachelor's degree, and graduating from arguably one of the world's finest law schools, he unfortunately remains legally blind. This story is a testament to him and others similarly disabled, that have courageously overcome life's obstacles, sometimes literally placed in their paths. With that said, I segue while digressing back to 1969, and the following vignette: Bruce H. was the totally blind, middle-aged neighbor who lived next door. He inhabited the old, unpainted, gray-colored, grungy, and rundown house, contrasted to our brand spanking new dwelling, on our dead-end street. I had seen him many times while we were constructing our home and could smell his presence by the cherry flavored pipe tobacco he was fond of smoking. Oftentimes he would whiz by our construction site, tapping his special red and white walking stick against the slate sidewalk, resembling a locomotive with white smoke billowing out of his pipe and mouth. He never stopped to talk, however, even though he knew we were building a house. That is until the day we were officially moved in. Let's back up first, however. Sure there were a few unfriendly syllables exchanged between my Grandpa Pete, Bruce, and his aged mother, while the building process was progressing, and sure there were more than a few skirmishes and insults hurled between my pop and Bruce regarding "grandfathered" property lines. Those border disputes were comical to witness but serious sounding at the same time. In addition to being a civil engineering professor, my father was also a licensed and gifted land surveyor. He had the deed in hand, all the correct instruments and surveyed the heck out of our property. When confronted by Bruce's mother, Mellen, he initially and carefully explained the "correct" boundaries betwixt our sloped, abutting lands. She had none of it and threatened to tell the "village people" that he was taking advantage of a locally well-known old lady and her blind son. Plus, she stated emphatically, she owned a gun and knew how to use it. However, no one drew a weapon but obviously "someone" could have, at any time, including my old man, who was well armed. Pop ignored her threats and continued the construction of our home. I believe he fudged his own data a bit to keep peace with her because ultimately nothing deleterious happened and all parties started speaking again. Paul B., the asthmatic, long retired man on the other side of our plot, never said a word about losing a few inches of lawn and laughingly told my dad that now he had less to mow. He and his wife, Hazel, turned out to be fantastic friends for my grandfather and decent neighborly people. Now, back to our main story: My dad and I were tossing handfuls of grass seed onto our future front lawn one late summer evening when Bruce stopped in our primitive unpaved driveway and proceeded to reload his pipe. We watched and waited, and waited some more. Usually he did his "tobacco business" elsewhere and sped by our property at a quick pace. This time he seemed eager for a chinwag. We obliged. Having been on friendly terms for a few months time now, my dad and I felt confident and approached him for some chitchat. We had never really gotten to know him, you know. With all that bad blood between us in the past, now was as good a time as any to become friends and finally bury the hatchet. He knew ALL about us, it seemed. The village morons and his mom had filled him in quite nicely. And much of his information was correct, too. But we weren't "damn Russians" my father repeatedly told him. I think it finally sunk in. He was thin, slightly hunched over, wore a cap, dark clothing, and wore thick spectacles. He quickly assured us that he could only see shapes, at best, and not always. He was a native son and had gradually grown sightless for years while memorizing the village and all its streets and shops. By fifteen years of age, he was totally blind. He grew up in the house next door that his deceased father had built decades ago. His elderly and cantankerous mother lived with him and they took care of one another at this point in their lives. He went on to say that he was starting an ice cream business and needed the slate sidewalk in front of our house to be as level as possible because of the cart he would soon be pulling over it. My father seemed amused at that pronouncement and assured him that all things would be smooth. We parted company and he zoomed away from us on the way to town. True to his word, pop made sure that all the large slate slabs were even with no lips to trip over or get a wheel stuck on. Shortly thereafter, we saw Bruce pull a refrigerated ice cream cart, heavily laden with treats, past our home and into the village, to peddle cones on street corners. That became a daily event in our town. Everyone knew him and lots of folks stopped by to chat and buy a morsel of cold, creamy, goodness. And he made a few bucks to supplement his Social Security checks. I watched him rapidly differentiate between coins by feel. How he handled paper money I do not know. He commenced those daily trips while crossing numerous streets and negotiated twisting roadways and hilly terrain. He admitted to us on a few occasions that he did have a few close calls with cars and that maybe he should acquire a Seeing Eye dog and ditch his stick once and for all. In the meantime, he encouraged my sister and me to go into his house for our ice cream needs and buy "freezer fresh" Sealtest brand desserts directly from his mother. I was scared of her. But by the fall, my sister and I were regular weekly customers, with frosty chocolate and butter pecan samplings being our weaknesses. Mellen H. was a short, snaggle-toothed, grizzled, wisp of a women with gnarly yellowed fingernails and white locks of hair with tinges of yellow in it. She spoke in a hillbilly inspired twang as if she had just arrived from Appalachia country. Her fierce blue eyes pierced right through you and seemed to denote a continously hardscrabble life, obviously not of her choosing. I would knock on the door, enter the musty, old-fashioned parlor, pick the carton of ice cream from the large horizontal freezer, pay the lady and leave, as quickly as possible. However, one Saturday afternoon I lingered and looked around at the faded photos present while my sister was making up her mind as to what flavor she desired. I saw many framed pictures of a young, blonde beauty. That couldn't be her, I thought. Some sleuthing among the village gossipmongers by my also curious mom divulged some interesting factoids: In her prime, Mellen

H. had been employed as a chambermaid in the town's largest and most ornate hotel, and was considered a real *looker*, as the menfolk would say. Also, rumor had it that many married men of means fancied her attractive features and lively spirit. But, alas, she married a ne'er-do-well carpenter that died young, had one child and lived with him in near poverty the rest of her life. Gone were her charms and prettiness; only her wicked wiles survived. When I met her, she was near the end of her tragic life. Bruce, on the other hand, kept on trucking and secured himself a Seeing Eye dog in the fall of '69. Rip was the name of his new golden Labrador retriever. Bruce had gone away prior, for six weeks, to train with him at a special site and returned home with his doggy charge. What a sight it was to see: the obedient dog pulling Bruce's right hand while he was struggling to pull the ice cream cart with his left. Nobody laughed and people gave him quarter to maneuver at will. However, Rip had a bad habit and I knew about it. Many times, as Bruce would stop for a quick verbal visit, I quickly found a stick and gave it to the dog. Bruce forbade us to fondle or pet him but let us give him sticks to chew. Rip would contentedly crunch them up and look for more. It was a rather tame vice for a Seeing Eye dog to have. Nevertheless, he trusted and loved his blind owner, you could just tell. The reverse was not always true, at least not in the beginning. One day in late October my family and I perceived the distinct odor of skunk cologne emanating from Bruce's yard and witnessed his usual clothing draped over a large branch of a blue spruce near the porch. He must have been skunked! Well, the way Bruce embarrassingly retold it, it seemed that while returning home and walking up a steep incline at dusk one night, his dog veered left while Bruce arrogantly tugged on the special leash to have him go straight. Bruce won the tug of war and practically stepped on the skunk in his way. The dog wanted to go around it but obeyed his master to the bitter end. Both got sprayed. After that debacle, Bruce said he implicitly trusted that yellow lab with his life. Years went by with Bruce regularly taking the dog into his cinder-filled back yard to urinate and defecate, next to the crumbling old outhouse and numerous failing and sagging sheds. His mother had passed and he soldiered on alone. The cinders were from his wood-burning stove. I don't think he had central heating in his home, it was that old. Rip eventually retired to a dog farm and, as I was leaving for college, another friendly canine appeared at his side. Lobo, a black and frisky lab, was now the point man. Bruce had retired from his supplemental ice cream business but continued his daily jaunts into town, smoking, and being led by a new companion. Bruce and I were never really close, or even pals, but I learned patience, forbearance and willpower from him. Maybe I instilled those same qualities in my legally blind son without realizing it. As a visually handicapped young man, I hope he continues to forge ahead in life without quitting. Thanks Bruce H. for your many *insights*.

65

Animal Stories

By now it had become quite evident to me that I loved
and was fully engrossed in naturalistic activities, willingly
having my elderly Clinton Street mentor, Dr. R., guide my
fertile mind with his entomological wisdom and old-
fashioned pastorly axioms. But it wasn't my full-time job; I
still attended school fulltime! My mother returned one
afternoon quite excited after visiting a rummage sale, or
was it a garage sale? Maybe the same thing? Anyway,
when I got home from school I saw three rather "old"
books on my bedroom dresser, all written by Thornton W.
Burgess. Mother peeked around my bedroom door as I
delicately handled the ancient texts and she left smiling,
when I smiled. They were hard cover originals, from the
early 1900s, with handwritten dedications and notes
scribbled inside. But they were discarded, picked up by my
mom for pennies. Were they any good? I'll say. Thornton
W. Burgess was best known as a beloved author of
children's books about animals and nature. His whimsical
style and anthropomorphism of animals instilled curiosity
among young readers and kept their interests to learn
about common critters. And, he hooked me rather

quickly. Here I was, a devoted science stud and reader of *National Geographic Magazine*, my encyclopedia volumes, and *Tell Me Why* books, and now *Mother West Wind "When" Stories*? Peter Rabbit, Grandfather Frog, The Merry Little Breezes and Johnny Chuck? What was wrong with me? Was I slipping backwards? Did I have a brain fart? I read *Highlights magazine* and *Reader's Digest* with a smirk and a yawn but those books by Burgess were a hoot, and I kept reading and rereading his mesmerizing and engaging chapters. Granted it was light reading but the subject matter was accurate, although slightly corny, with human attire, foibles, and characteristics thrown in. However I deeply treasured those books. Mom was pleased with her paltry purchases and I thanked her for them. Supplemented with television's Sunday nights' *Mutual of Omaha's Wild Kingdom* with Marlin Perkins, Burgess's books, and my own local nature adventures, proved to me where my passions lay. Fast forward three decades or so: my naturalist daughter was the recipient of those same books, and more that I had ordered online. She also loved them. Jimmy Skunk, Sammy Jay, Ole' Mistah Buzzard, etc., became her personal friends and came "alive" in her bedroom. Besides reading journals such as *Highlights, My Big Backyard, Cricket and Kaatskill Life magazine* (which we both wrote for, for decades), my nature-leaning female offspring made zoology her passion, vocation and, ultimately, career. She earned a Ph.D. in Ecology and Evolutionary Biology, having done a doctoral dissertation on dagger moths. Was it all because of Bobby Coon and Tommy Trout in Burgess's books? Was it because she grew up in her own big backyard, with a pond, with my tutelage and similar love of nature? All of the above? It's funny how certain timely events can shape a life.

Take a break!

FIFTH GRADE

66

Penmanship Counts?

Mrs. C. was the prototypical schoolmarm. Stern,
bespectacled, and "old-fashioned," she was a crotchety old
biddy. But she knew enough about child psychology to
keep we students coming back for more, day after day. She
knew when to push, when to punish and when to back off,
to get the best out of us. She was a clever and talented
teacher, even though an *old lady*. Her big bid in our fifth
grade classroom was teaching us how to *properly* write in
longhand. The precise forms for all the letters of the
alphabet were plastered around the room, just under the
ceiling. If you forgot how to write a capital F, for instance,
there it was, above the blackboard. Even then most kids
cursed at cursive writing, especially because Mrs. C.
devoted so much time to it. It was a tedious and
frustrating daily class chore. She would slowly recite a
simple passage and we would start writing it down. Then
she would methodically pass through our rows of desks and
correct our postures, hand positions, pen-holding grips,
and slant of the letters and words. Left-handers suffered
because she didn't know what to do with them. While
being sympathetic to the few southpaws present, she

nevertheless berated them harshly because their letters were frequently poorly formed and slanted the *wrong* way. She was definitely "old school." What can I say? Luckily I was right-handed. So I learned to print in first grade and how to *write* in fifth. I did receive all the coveted class awards for my penmanship endeavors, and was proud to show them to my family members. However, my father, a gifted calligrapher and artist, scoffed at my efforts and rewards. My "feeble, squiggly attempts at writing," as he called it, were barely passable in his book. Oh, boy. As usual, I was not measuring up to HIS lofty standards again. I never could, and never will. Oh, well. Contrast that with my own son. Growing up in the computer generation, his keyboarding and gaming abilities are great but he can barely print or sign his name. I would peek at his unintelligible notebooks from college and shake my head in disbelief. How could he read his own shitty class notes? Here was a prep school valedictorian, an Ivy League and top law school educated grown man that would gingerly clasp a writing implement as if it was a prickly and poisonous botanical offshoot. He perceived a pen to be a nasty foreign object that didn't belong in his grasp. However, instead of feeling ashamed or guilty, he exalted in his inability to write. And my dad, while deriding ME long ago, also glorified his smart grandson and his lack of writing prowess. What gives? Either my old man mysteriously mellowed with age or my son had buffaloed him in some way. Was I chopped liver, or what? I just can't win.

67

Lenny and George

My fifth grade class took working in bunches to a new level. And if we weren't in large groups, at least we had a choice of partner to complete tasks in the social sciences. The rest of the subjects were usually solo affairs and harshly graded by old Mrs. C. But when it came time for history and social studies, her scholastic standards dropped slightly and we were allowed to study, research, learn, and present as foursomes, threesomes, or twosomes. Early in the school year, M.S., a rather burly, and tall farm boy, glommed onto me, academically speaking. And I couldn't shake him, well, he WAS much bigger than me. We traveled in different socioeconomic, intellectual, athletic, and friendship circles but when it was time for a two-man project, he magically appeared at my side. He was polite and soft-spoken; a gentle giant at heart, regardless of his behemoth status. I couldn't say no. It got to the point where Mrs. C. assumed we were a perpetual team, even before I could utter a protest. Oh, well. Thus, in her class that school year, Lenny and George were reborn (from the Steinbeck book *Of Mice and Men*). I did the heavy mental lifting and talking, while he was the "heavy" in the elementary school library. We ALWAYS got the books we needed before anyone else in our class. He made sure of it, or else. Of course we BOTH received A's as a dynamic duo. During the required class presentations, I would nod to him while orating as he solemnly sat next to me in front of the class. The teacher smiled with a twinkle in her good eye; she knew what was going on. But, hey, perhaps he learned SOMETHING from me, and maybe HE was cunningly clever after all, letting ME do most of the work?! Who was really the smarter guy?

68

Overdue Blues

What began as a gentle verbal jibing by the elementary school librarian turned into a weekly shaming session in front of my peers in the grades 4-6 school library. And it continued unabated, making my life miserable. All because of an overdue library book that she claimed I had never returned. Not only was I allegedly tardy, she made me out to be a thief, with no conscience. I was clueless as to how her vitriol toward me quickly spiraled out of control. I recollect checking the book out normally, reading it and then returning it, as I had done previously with dozens of other volumes. No big deal, right? However, somehow this particular book went missing in action, and I was the last one to have physically touched it. Mrs. P. would have our class sit around a large oval wooden table at the beginning of each weekly library hour, make announcements, and teach we uninterested dummies about library science. She would end each talk by mentioning me and my delinquency. True dat, but what did I ever do to her? I told her multiple times that I didn't have the book! I was embarrassed, my buddies looked confused and she was relentless. I probably could have asked my parents to buy her the book but my pride and principles were injured. Her obsessive and unwarranted remarks toward me continued weekly, for months; it became somewhat of a running bad joke after a while, with me being the perpetual patsy. Finally, I told my teacher, Mrs. C., about my alleged transgression and innocence. She must have intervened because soon after, Mrs. P. stopped accusing me of petit larceny and I ceased being the heel in her squared circle. To my knowledge, no one ever fessed up to the crime or returned the publication. I guess the book was never found. If someone had deliberately nicked it just to goof on me, then she/he succeeded. Those few months were anguishing times for me and I nervously began to dread the mandatory weekly library junkets. Hopefully a weisenheimer got a good laugh at my expense. If not, then the book was actually gone. Maybe Mrs. P. unintentionally misfiled it and it was there all along? Perhaps, but say it ain't so!

69

The Cafeteria Caper

It appeared that L. J.'s inner time bomb was ticking silently all this time. Who knew? Being a small (K-3) school, we all knew each other and would play together on the playground at recess. However, he was only an acquaintance of mine at best. But by third grade, students in the know, like me, realized that he had been held back. Now he was one of "them." Second grade had not been overwhelming but was obviously not kind to him. He had failed it. He was also known as somewhat of a hothead and didn't like to be pushed around. We all knew how he was. Now, suddenly he boiled over. All the teasing and insinuations must have finally provoked his inner rage that fateful lunch period when he was a fourth grader and we, fifth graders. The processional to get the eats started as usual that noon. The fourth, fifth and sixth graders lined up in the chow line in the long hallway leading up to the cafeteria door. I noticed L.J. in line with the rest of his fourth grade compatriots up ahead. He was a whole head taller than they; he was taller than most of the sixth graders as well! Then the usual daily ribbing from the same bunch of fifth graders started in and from some of his former close friends, no less. You know the comments and snide remarks that were usually uttered: "Hey, Louis, you doofus! Hey, Louis, did you fail two grades or one? Hey, Louis, leave some grub for us." Much cackling and self-congratulatory backslapping accompanied those inflammatory insults as they were thrown out by those heckling bullies. Meanwhile, he turned red in shame and anger, because everyone around knew that he was the mark. His fists were clenched and he was seething. You could just feel it. But there were teachers around. He calmed down because he had to. Sure, he had antagonized some of those guys in K-2, and now they thought the tables were turned in their favor. Of course none of those weaseley cowards dared to confront him face-to-face. Of course not. Just a few choice, loud, and obnoxious catcalls were lobbed his way to get his dander up. So on this particular day we loaded up our trays with nutritious but inauspicious looking foodstuffs and settled in with our mates to start nibbling and munching. No sooner did we have some bland morsels in our cake-holes, when L. J. came strolling over to those fifth grade assholes that were mercilessly riding him. He was mad and disheveled, but he kind of always looked that way. He grabbed their cafeteria table and tipped it over. He finally turned the tables on them! They were stunned and motionless. Then he proceeded to pick up the chunks of cottage cheese, pineapple slices, and Sloppy Joe's from the shiny linoleum floor and started to pelt his tormentors. It all happened so fast. The rest of us were startled and just watched, mesmerized. Teachers quickly intervened and escorted him to the principal's office. The whole dramatic affair lasted less than five minutes, but had a lasting effect on those teasing dolts. Looking back now, I think some of them should have been held back as well. Also, that was the era of physical fighting, not gunplay. In today's world, Louis might have brought in his old man's firearms and killed some kids. Back in those days, we all had easy access to various guns and bullets, but violent shit like killings didn't happen. We all got lucky. Well, nothing untoward happened to L.J. and things simmered back to "normal" the next day. And nothing was ever hurled after that food exchange, either hurtful words or hot dogs. During successive lunches, I purposely moved up in line and sidled up to L.J., and we started a rapport again. He was elated to talk to an "upperclassman;" actually from the grade he should have been in. I was happy to have a *tough* guy for a friend. I never knew when I would have to drop his name to get out of a schoolyard scrape. You just never knew when Mowgli would need the timely intervention of Baloo the Bear. You just never knew.

70

Bored Games

Rainy weekends were the worst. After pounding out some Czerny and Brahms on the ivories during piano practice, sketching a few odds and ends with a charcoal pencil, and reading a bunch of pages in my latest *Tell Me Why* book, by Arkady Leokum, I was still bored. Maybe I should have badgered my sister to play some real board games with me? Nah, she was too little, and I hurriedly teased her to tears. You know, that's what older siblings did. Nevertheless, I was restless. I would get inventive whenever there were no obligatory adult indoor projects to waste my time on. I used my initiative, if you will. I would close and lock my bedroom door, quickly inventory my stock of toys, and get busy. I never whined or complained and could play well by myself for hours at a time, with my existing fleet of goods. The Creepy Crawlers set would invariably come out, complete with some new plates and new hued Goop bottles I had purchased at our downtown Western Auto store. Of course as soon as the telltale odor of curing rubbery latex wafted through our upstairs, my sister would come pounding on my door to let her in and join me in the creative fun. I couldn't say no as she enthusiastically started pouring her own plates. I was in charge of baking, cooling and separating our multicolored, *creepy*, and monstrous works of art. Well that lasted an hour or so. Now what? I guessed it was time to do some shootin' and to carefully practice my line of fire. Sis left as I cleaned up the Creepy Crawlers setup, boxed the cooled down oven and carefully stowed it away, next to my realistic looking plastic pistols that fired plastic bullets. I lined up my "enemy" army men, plastic jeeps and tanks, and pretending to be General George S. Patton, launched the attack. Sure I missed sometimes, but not often. I seemed to be genetically predisposed with good aim, a very steady hand and a non twitchy trigger finger. My present day dental skills are of no surprise to me for I had unwittingly trained my eyes, hands and fingers years prior. Who knew that toy guns, bullets and shooting would be so beneficial for my future as a dentist? Well, the good guys won and took over the whole territory, the top of my bed. Now what? Clean up and move on to toy trucks, including my S&H Green Stamps-purchased Tonka Jeep winch-truck? Perhaps some car racing instead? Now don't get me wrong; I don't have ADHD and really DID savor all the moments of playing. But I liked to keep things moving, myself included. I set up the ten-foot-long segmented length of plastic track from the top of my tallest dresser, over my bed and ending on the floor. I unpacked my special *Hot Wheels* carrying case and disgorged dozens of the miniaturized reproduction vehicles onto my hardwood floor. Some were genuine Mattel *Hot Wheels* products, some were *Matchbox* cars, made by Lesney, in Britain. The two sets of tiny cars and trucks were similar, except for the wheels. *Hot Wheels* had oversized tires and springy suspensions while the Lesney-brand miniatures had proportional wheels and shock absorbency. Basically, the *Hot Wheels* were faster, but I ran the test runs regularly, just to make sure. I didn't have a stopwatch so the second hand on my watch had to do. Each vehicle got a fair chance to race down the inclined plastic track as I logged in the time of finish. Of course my *Hot Wheels* purple and black '68 Chevy El Camino bested my *Matchbox* cobalt blue Lotus Europa by a few seconds every time. They were my fastest cars. Once I got into the "car" mood, I would often set up my figure 8 grooved, electrified track and invite my sister over to race our two specially modified track cars with fist-held throttles. The set came with two autos, a white '65 Ford Mustang and a bright red '65 Chevy Impala. I quickly realized that the Impala fishtailed while cornering and frequently went of course, regardless of the guardrails. I made that one my sister's car. I drove the stubby Mustang to victory almost every time. Oh well, at least she got a chance to stop dressing up those boring Barbie and Stacy dolls, and dropped them to play with her older brother. She never complained about losing. Ha. But my thumb became quite sore from depressing that primitive joystick as we played for an hour or so. The afternoon and rain had passed, as did the weekend. I sadly packed all my wheeled gadgets away and washed up for supper. But I was still wired, and my heart whizzing, from all the racing I had done on my bedroom floor and in my imagination. Maybe a quiet puzzle or board game should have been played with instead? No way.

71

Premature Jock Itch

Sexually separated physical education (P.E.) was deemed necessary for both girls and boys, even in our rinky-dink rural school district. Needless to say, gym was one of my best loved classes. I had already regularly started smacking tennis and table tennis balls with my father, depending on the season, and began to feel confident in my athletic prowess. At age ten, I could more than hold my own against the bigger but premature jocks in my grade, much to the chagrin and consternation of our new gym teacher. Being an alumnus, and the varsity football, basketball, and track coach, he was always actively on the lookout for sports potential in the elementary school grades. We were his minor leaguers. Once he determined his "winners," he would be itching to blatantly *groom* his little "jocks" for future varsity positions and possibly Di college stardom. How dare a scrawny, quick, coordinated, brown-skinned, black-haired boy outshine his "chosen athletes?" Nevertheless, I frequently did. What transpired in gym was obvious discrimination, at least it was obvious to me. And unfair. His favorites were always anointed by him to be squad leaders, were handpicked first to be taught a particular exercise, received the highest marks, etc. The other physically average fifth graders just assumed their positions and took it. They only went through the motions. They instinctively knew the predetermined athletic pecking order by age ten and meekly accepted their B averages without an ounce of protestation. Not me. I was getting B's for A-plus work in the gym. Wtf? It's interesting that I was picked first for dodgeball or for any team by the squad leaders; my sports abilities were well-known among my peers, just willfully ignored by the gym teacher. I knew I wasn't one of HIS "boys," nor did I try to be in their clique. I just wanted some respect and to be graded fairly. I could run faster, aim well, and catch balls better than most of his jocks-in-training. My mother finally got tired of my carping and went to a meeting with him. She said, "Does my Izzy just stand there like a numbskull, drop all the balls and cower in fear?" "No ma'am," replied Mr. K. "Didn't Izzy just win the 400-yard dash?" "Yes ma'am," stammered Mr. K. "Isn't Izzy the first boy picked for dodgeball?" she implored. "Yes," replied the now red-faced teacher. "So, why is he getting such lousy grades in gym?" she demanded. Mr. K. was fuming. His volatile Irish temper boiled over but then quickly receded as he must have thought about the situation some more. In halting, measured sentences, he assured my mother that in the future he would keep an extra eye on me and my gymnasium performances, as he put it. I had to believe her story about the confrontation because suddenly my grades shot up. I still wasn't a favorite son to Mr. K., but I didn't care. My grades now accurately reflected my athleticism and he could no longer turn a biased and bigoted eye to that. So I ended up with A's in P.E. through my senior year, and with different instructors. I deserved it. But thanks, Mom, for stirring the pot and leveling the playing field in my favor all those years ago. I know I'm YOUR favorite son; actually your ONLY son. What a mom!

72

Ponce de León

It was time for a rare solo social studies project involving ancient explorers. After expounding on that topic for a week, Mrs. C. asked we fifth graders to choose a *discoverer* from the extensive list she had posted next to the blackboard. I quickly picked my favorite: Ponce de León. I liked his cool sounding name. We had to research and write a short piece about our chosen explorer. Although already aware of him, now was my chance to fully indulge my fantasies and imagine what it was like being a brave conquistador in the early 1500s. It would be a labor of love, and it turned out to be so. I also received an easy A for my efforts. Bonus. Historically rumored to be searching for the "Fountain of Youth" in Florida, Ponce de León was in fact a noted aristocrat from a noble family, and a soldier of fortune. He was subsequently appointed by the Spanish king as the first governor of a newly subdued and subjugated territory: Puerto Rico. While later putting down a native rebellion in southwestern Florida, he was mortally wounded by a poisoned arrow and died in Cuba in 1521. That ends the quickie history lesson, or does it? What was there not to admire about him? A legendary conqueror and adventurer, right? Well, "history" in my elementary school was severely truncated and taught with a chauvinistic and western European tilt. Okay, so the Aztecs, Incas, and Mayas were also described but they received short shrift compared to other populations and figures deemed more important to learn about. But what about the Tainos and Caribs, whose Caribbean islands were virtually pulled out from under them by overly zealous, greedy, and plundering Europeans? Under the guise of righteous piety and "God-given" Manifest Destiny, indigenous tribes were decimated and basically forgotten about as expediently as possible. Obviously today we have become much more sensitive, archeologically and paleontologically better educated, and more "politically correct" in our often revisionist approach to that long-ago era. But in fifth grade, Ponce was *my boy*; he was *the Man*. Strong and determined, he fought and defeated "savage" Native Americans as easily as an afterthought. Those "pesky" original people were a thorn in his backside and needed to be eradicated, and most were. I bought it all and believed what I learned. Now granted, you cannot cover everything in class and there was no time for dissent or opposing viewpoints. I also did not attend an expensive private prep school or even a misguided Montessori school. My public grammar school teachers were under constraints to teach and preach the gospel, western European dogma, with just a smattering about other religions, cultures and faraway lands thrown in. Much later, in high school, Marco Polo would surface, as well as the middle east, China and India. However, for now we were stuck in the western hemisphere. So was Ponce a pillager, a ruthless murderer, and a privileged pompous twit? Perhaps. Was he also an officer of the Spanish Crown, a land grabber, governor, and war hero? Most assuredly. Did he exterminate the locals to allow for the complete colonization of Puerto Rico by Spain? You betcha. Too bad that those early social studies and history courses could not have been taught with kernels of truth thrown in to at least force us to think and form our own hypotheses and conclusions. On the other hand, too much ruminating and differences of opinion would have led to educational anarchy. How could you answer a test question if there were always two logical sides to the same story? Anyway, perhaps the least we can now do is to celebrate Native American Day in lieu of Columbus Day. I know, too little, too late. And I should be grateful because lots of Europe's progeny would not be settled in the Americas today if the De Sotos, Hudsons and Magellans had been thwarted by more of those poisoned arrows back then. Who knows?

73

Snowballs from Heaven

How did I find myself temporarily incarcerated in elementary school principal Ralph H.'s office, bewildered, bundled up, sweating bullets in my winter attire, and surrounded by four of my closest pals? Boy, were we frightened. It was my first and only time officially *sent* to the principal's office. But I was innocent I tell you. I was a victim of circumstance! So why was I sitting in a melting puddle of slush, on the *hot seat*, in his overheated office, with crumpled cakes of snow slowly falling off of me? His office became an oven while he methodically and malevolently interrogated each of us in turn. He was old, cold, calculating, and ready to administer corrective measures at a moment's notice. I was in major league trouble; let me explain. It was one of my buddies, or maybe it was I that instigated that minor and cockamamie melee on the snow-covered playground at recess that fateful day. Nevertheless, what genuinely transpired was NOT what one of the "stupid" playground monitors thought she saw happen. Yes, snowball fights were explicitly verboten and yes, we five idiots were guilty of making and gripping snowballs in our mitten-encased hands. However we were not flinging them at one another, or yelling, or crying out in pain. One of we bright bulbs thought it would be cool to see who could toss a snowball underhand to the highest distance above us. So we started making and chucking icy contraband skyward in unison, at specified intervals, and kept score of who was winning. Unfortunately, as we stood close together, our woolen hats and shoulders quickly became covered in broken snowballs that we could not dodge, ones that rained down on us from above. To a certain schoolyard monitor, it was a no-brainer. We were obviously snowball fighting. Technically, we were not, but were "caught" red-handed by her nonetheless. She gleefully rounded us up and told us to immediately start walking up to the elementary school building because we had caused a gross infraction (what?!) and needed to be punished by the principal. We loudly chimed in at once protesting our innocence and tried valiantly to explain ourselves. She would have none of it as she herded us like sheep to continue the death march. Crap. How could this have happened? Violating a major rule, no less. It sounded so despicable and disturbing. And what would the punishment be? I had heard that Mr. H. was a meanie and even had a reputation for making misbehaving male lawbreakers bawl. Even his secretary, Mrs. R., was a beaut. But wait, nothing happened. Honest Injun. Principal H.

looked us over, scowled broadly, and gravely shook his head in our general direction. He knew full well we were some of the "good" kids in our grade that mainly forsook tomfoolery for studiousness. He gave us a break, chuckled warmly, and dismissed us with a smirk on his face. And he was right to trust us without having to mete out any discipline. We never again made another snowball on school property. We silently trundled back down to the playing field with that same jovial monitor in the lead. I certainly would have enjoyed giving that nearsighted old bag the sack, but I had no such authority to do so. I hated her, and still do. Now it was time to return to class. I exhaled deeply as I peeled off my winter clothing and boots, and slumped down heavily onto my wooden seat. It had been a close call that day and I was relieved to have been so quickly acquitted. So were my friends. Case closed.

74

Religious Freedom and Music

My Podunk village was barren of a lot of "standard" amenities, such as a bowling alley, a movie theater, adequate gray matter among the local populace, and any churches with the words "Christian Orthodox" emblazoned on the front door. Mind you, our town boasted a heady bevy of Christian denominations and even some evangelical congregations. But there was nothing for we Eastern European "foreigners." Of course, if my family had been adamant, we could have traveled weekly to distant cities to meet "our own kind," to satisfy our unique Christian heritage, and worship at will. But my dad was not motivated to do that. And he had the keys to the car. Or perhaps he was secretly a cynical nonbeliever and evolving atheist? Who knows? I never questioned him, but I suspected the latter. Therefore my sister and I were raised with distant religious roots that were no longer anchored to a specific church. We became freethinkers, unencumbered by ANY religious dogma. Amen. As the only "talented" male pupil of my piano teacher, I felt special, and it was not lost on her. She flaunted my sex as a marketing gimmick around town, at every chance, to garner more piano students for her stable. Not only was I a decent keyboardist, but I also liked to perform in public. Ironically, I was frequently asked to stroke the ivories, with appropriate selections, on many Sundays in area churches during the services. Although I had no organized religion of my own, there I was, banging away at the black and whites at the Methodist, Presbyterian, Baptist and Episcopal houses of the holy. I never played at the Catholic church; Father R. had never asked me to. However, the others all relished my musical abilities and frequent visits. I would finish up my pieces, pack up my notes, bow and then sit politely and respectfully through psalms, hymns, homilies, songs, chants, and words of *wisdom*. Hundreds of such recitals commenced during my fifth grade year to "harden" me and make me a respectable public performer. It was a cunning plan by my piano instructor to get me prepared for NYSSMA (New York State School Music Association) competitions. It was all the musical rage back in the day. NYSSMA this, NYSSMA that. She set the stage, and I delivered. Four perfect NYSSMA scores in four consecutive years that were locally publicized brought me a modicum of musical notoriety, and many new students, including boys, for her. A win-win, I guess. Strangely, though, none of my continuous and copious rubbing of shoulders with the

Almighty in his various "houses" ever corrupted my mind to capitulate to Him, or to any higher power. Funny how that worked out, or didn't.

75

Piano Man?

To keep her small cadre of mostly female piano students motivated and provide proof of progress to the parents, my locally well-known Eastman School of Music trained teacher signed us up yearly for the New York State School Music Association "competitions" for grades l-Vl level music. They were held annually in a nearby city university to great fanfare and notoriety, if you were into that kind of stuff, that is. The common folk of my village probably barely noticed the "importance" of NYSSMA. I admit I was one of the pompous sorts that reveled in my official designation as a participant. All New York State school instrumentalists, singers, vocal ensembles, orchestras, choirs, and bands were invited to attend the weeklong affair, during specified times, to be adjudicated and given a letter grade. It wasn't really a competitive event; music students competed against themselves. Achieving an A rating for a three-part test was the ultimate goal in my day. For piano, the three parts consisted of scaling two major scales in three octaves, sight-reading a previously unseen set of notes, and then performing a memorized piece of music to perfection. The panel of three female/male adjudicators were definitely not The Three Stooges but somber, well-trained musicians, with no senses of humor while judging we plebes. It was rough enough existing as a fifth grader, and then being kowtowed to grind away at the black and whites like a monkey to get a grade. Not a prize, or money, but a lousy letter of the alphabet. Who really cared? My parents? My teacher? Was I a chimp or a chump? Perhaps both? And this was after a year of rigorous daily practice to get my Level ll piano composition up to Mrs. M.'s standard of excellence, prior to the NYSSMA extravaganza. However, I lived to compete, be it in sports, scholastically, or on the piano. I relished being one of the few male piano students in our village and arrogantly enjoyed being known as a piano player. Our busload of would-be virtuosos arrived early on that dreary Saturday in March. I saw my name posted next to the piano room and anxiously awaited my turn. Then into the special room designated as the "piano chamber" went Mrs. M. and me. She accompanied each of her pupils, and now it was my turn to get grilled. This was my first time, darn it. Was I prepared? Well, I was prepared to eat lunch; my mom had made some great sandwiches for me. But to play well in front of stern strangers? I wasn't so sure. I was Mrs. M.'s youngest NYSSMA "volunteer" and only boy. Of course I was attired in a handsome zoot suit, complete with polished black shoes, white shirt and tie. I briskly walked to the Steinway, past the peering judges, and adjusted the bench, just as Mrs. M. quietly took her own seat in a corner of the spacious and soundproof room. I sat down impassively as if an old hand at this, leaned forward, listened intently to the judges' directions, and played my heart out. Sure, I had sweaty palms and butterflies in my belly, but I fearlessly attacked those ivories with measured gusto, while being scrupulously scrutinized by the judicial trio, which had prior been handed copies of my musical selection. I finished, bowed and exited. The unemotional and usually standoffish Mrs. M. grabbed me in the hallway and awkwardly hugged up on me. Sure enough, I received an A for my efforts with multiple positive comments from the judges. It was only grade ll music, but still.... I was elated and relieved, kind of like after winning a race. But piano playing was supposed to be a fun hobby, not a chore. Or was it? I was no prodigy but felt prodded like one. All those church rehearsals and recitals to toughen me up had worked wonderfully. All those hours of sometimes frustrating practice had correctly molded my fingers as well. I had been adequately prepared and nailed it. But how did all that happen? Why did it all start in the first place? My mom could play a little and started me off at age four. It was FUN and I quickly surpassed my old lady at our old Winter upright. Witnessing that I possessed some skills, she signed me up for lessons with THE local piano teacher, Mrs. M., whose husband taught at the same college as my dad and whose daughter was in my grade. I officially started lessons by age six on Saturday mornings, at the Second Presbyterian Church, with my mother already fancifully thinking I would be the next Liberace or Van Cliburn. NOT. My house began to be filled with pretentious classical and operatic recordings because that's what I was learning and my folks thought that's the way things should be. Very highbrow. They didn't count on me being somewhat of a lowbrow *mensch* when it involved tunage. Rock-and-roll, the Beatles, and even Karen Carpenter were outlawed for fear of corrupting my Beethoven-esque touch and having me turn to the dark side of music. By fourth grade I was coming along nicely, according to Mrs. M. Being her only male pupil with an ounce of talent, she pushed me, with NYSSMA always looming on the horizon. NYSSMA was like figure skating at the Olympics – you practiced like crazy to get one shot at the gold. No do-overs, no second chances. It was an A or nothing in her book. There was lots of pressure on me to compete and excel, but at the piano? Give me a break. I already had sports, why did piano have to continue to be this way? I enjoyed learning new pieces but detested all the theory and constant preparation that was required for the annual tournament. Eighth grade found me playing at level IV but enjoying Elton John and Scott Joplin more than Chopin and Liszt. My sister began lessons and we played a few duets at recitals. She was a good student and also advanced rapidly. By eleventh grade I had enough, switching teachers to be able to play for pleasure again. Kind of like switching coaches in tennis. Sometimes you just had to do it. But during my active playing days I had earned four A's, and gaudy medals, at four consecutive NYSSMA events and reached grade V music. After endless lessons at the church and later, weekly, after school at Mrs. M.'s house, on her upright Yamaha, enough was enough. Laid-back and mousey Mrs. L., my new teacher, appreciated my acumen and continued my lessons, but mainly in a contemporary instead of classical mode. Before my senior year ended I retired from lessons and piano altogether. I was done. I realized I had become a skilled technician, not a musician. It also was hard for me to acknowledge that piano had become such a big part of my life, with little to show for my efforts. It was truly shameful that I could read notes well but not play by ear or improvise a tune. No amount of extra practice would instill that special "musicianship quality" in me, no matter how hard I tried. Either you had it or you didn't. I didn't. I currently own a beautiful, black, Yamaha baby grand, but rarely play anymore. I had started my children with homegrown lessons that were relatively quickly abandoned. They had no love for the instrument although my daughter did participate in ONE NYSSMA competition. One was enough for her. She quit playing shortly thereafter. I failed as a piano man, as a piano instructor, and failed to live up to my mom's expectations. Sorry, mom, and Mrs. M. Nevertheless, I still savor the fleeting musical triumphs from my past youth and being known around town and in school as a lad that could "really play," but I had limited musicality and no real talent. Sad. I can still scale, however.

76

Girls Rule?

My pals considered me a fast runner and an all-around athlete, even at ten years of age. My then gym teacher begrudgingly acknowledged as much, but only after a tongue-lashing by my mom. I wasn't a typical jock however; at least I had half a brain. I was feeling mighty happy and proud that school year and was proceeding along swimmingly. I had a high classroom average, had impressed my teacher Mrs. C. with my science acumen, and reveled in my status as a sportsman. Then came the rub, dammit. A smarty-pants girl that I did not know, another fifth grader I presumed, came right up to me on the playground at recess one warm spring day and told me she was faster than I. Some other girls in my class seemed to know her so I figured she was my age. She stood a head taller than me and had long legs. But didn't she know about my sporty accomplishments? Didn't she know that I had recently won the fifth grade boys 400-yard dash? She had some gall to challenge me in front of my buddies, right out in the open. Boastfully, I accepted. What else could I do? Sounds like the Old West. When the sheriff got challenged, he had to either put up and draw, or leave town in disgrace. I decided to put up and run. Word spread fast. In no time we had the large grassy playground set up for a roughly 50-yard sprinting showdown. I thought this would be easy. It was only 50 yards. We stood at the start area as she swept back her long brown hair and adjusted her billowy dress. A large gauntlet of kids stood watching and cheering, mainly for me. We took off when my buddy M.S. said go. I lost, and by a lot. No matter that I was the fastest boy, I was clearly not the fastest fifth grader. My hype had been better than my legs. My stunned friends all gathered around me looking confused and conciliatory. She was beaming and chatty with the other girls but not derogatory toward me in any way. She had wanted to prove a point, and she did. We never shook hands, however. Some of the boys did holler out that it wasn't a fair race because she was bigger than me. I said nothing; I was still in shock. How did she beat me? And with a dress on, no less. Recess ended, classes ended, and she ended up transferring out of our school after fifth grade. But even though I never knew her name, that humiliating defeat forever galvanized my resolve to be honest about my physical abilities and not buy into my own hyperbole too much. I'm glad I lost; it made me a humble and hungry athlete, up until today. Nevertheless, girls ARE more mature than boys in the fifth grade. There, I said it.

77

Smile!

I don't know what it was about my family. We already
touched upon the subject of "joy." Spontaneous levity was
frowned upon for fear of jinxing the future. You laugh,
then invariably you weep. But if you went about your
business even-keeled and dour, without highs and lows,
then you wouldn't set yourself up for disappointments or
sadness. Well that was my family's internal credo, and I
adhered to it, as best as I could. Although underneath my
front was a comic just bursting to get out, and he
succeeded in bits and pieces, as time went on. However,
for now I had no choice but to frown for my annual class
pictures. But wait, what was that? Izzy brought home a
school portrait with a smirk on his face? No way. Way!
My folks and especially Grandpa Pete were horrified and
very dismayed. I mean, if you perused our photo albums,
there was no one smiling, no one laughing, just sourpuss
expressions, on bland faces, akin to the old-fashioned
lithograph subjects of the 1800s. It was too late to "correct"
my audacious mug on that school photo, but it was not
too late to reinforce our rigid photographical fiefty at
home. I forgot to mention in previous stories that in

addition to the host of odd jobs he had just prior to his escape to the New World, Grandpa Pete was also a part-time professional photographer in the old country. To make ends meet in his new country, he photographed Estonian weddings, baptisms and other immigrant-based events. Oh, he had the best equipment: Zeiss and Leica bellows-cameras, flashbulbs deluxe, backlighting, and multiple tripods to do his dirty work with. All in black and white, however. My "hideous" fifth grade school picture had sent him into the usual frenzy. Out came all the equipment; it was time to show the family that he still had it as a photographer. Yearly "portrait taking" of our family members usually happened on scheduled Sunday nights, but this time he was deadly serious and wanted to photograph us in a goddamn hurry! Of course the time selected was a Sunday evening, when my sister and I should have been watching Pinocchio, or Snow White, on the *Wonderful World of Disney*. Hours were spent posing my dressed-up sister and me. Swearwords and derogatory remarks in Estonian were freely bantered about by him. My sister and I were just not measuring up as serious models as he kept repeating his facetious catch phrase in his native tongue: smile! Yeah, right. Grandpa Pete furiously worked the multiple cameras focused on us with mom and pop helping to calm us down. My sister was in tears and I was close to a meltdown as the nightmare finally ended. But all the resulting pics justified the *old master*. Our faces looked as if we had just been liberated from a concentration camp, with sunken cheekbones and vacant looking, swollen eyes. Grandpa Pete developed the photos in our sophisticated cellar darkroom himself and felt vindicated as a topnotch photographer. My sister and I had missed another glorious Disney animated flick as my somber mom apologetically put us to bed. I wondered aloud how Grandpa Pete got paid by clients acting the way he did. Mother assured me that he was polite and deferential with cash paying strangers. He only took out his frustrations on his family. What frustrations? He was long retired, lived debt free in a beautiful village with my folks, had his own garden, even his own dark green Rambler American automobile. He also didn't smoke, drink, dance, nor chew. I guessed that it must have been his personal and lifelong psychological demons that continuously gnawed at him and were hard to suppress and deal with. In his mind, maybe the "Russians" WERE still after him? Nevertheless, none of those knee-jerk reaction, homegrown black and white photos made it into our family albums. Mother proudly displayed that school-bought, "smiling," fifth grade, colored shot of her Izzy, much to the continued chagrin and disapproval of my grandfather.

78

Woodchuck 101

Some human connoisseurs call them groundhogs, land beavers or whistle pigs, names which sound so hoity toity and noble. In our neck of the redneck woods, we called them woodchucks, a word presumably derived from the original Algonquin term for them: "wuchaks." They are pesky and stubborn subterranean rodents and are the bane of cattle farmers. Their holey homes can break a cow's leg if accidentally stepped into by an unwary bovine. Our new property abutted a large, grassy, hilly field that my sister and I would routinely traverse. There were no "No Trespassing" signs posted so we would crawl under the barbwire fencing and explore the slanted meadow. Besides searching for monarch butterfly eggs on the undersides of milkweed leaves, and catching our fill of winged insects, we were also PREPARED for our inevitable encounters with the telltale mounds of earth that demarcated a woodchuck's homestead. Prepared, you ask? Yes, we always came heavily armed with old, used, tennis balls slit open and filled with five to six large firecrackers apiece. It was a lot of fun lighting the long fuse and chucking a ball into a burrow. The tennis ball would disappear from view, then

BOOM! The ground would quiver for a second and then plumes of acrid, sulfurous smoke would pour out of the holes. There were always two entrances, a front and back door. But nobody got hurt. The tough underground mammal was probably annoyed at our prank, at best. Weeks later we would find the discarded and singed tennis balls outside the dirt piles next to the holes. Those were *normal* childhood summer adventures for us. You know: seeking out bugs and salamanders, swimming at the village pool, riding bikes on our new dead-end street, and throwing bombs down woodchuck holes.

79

Trippin'

When it came time for some hard-core grocery shopping, and not just veggies from our garden, the local food vendors sufficed; none of us went hungry that I know of. But if you desired to peruse and purchase sporting equipment, furniture, or indulge in some fine dining, you had to buckle yourself into a horseless carriage and *schlep* over hill and dale to the nearest city. However, OUR nearby city was barely one, but it did have the requisite universities, fast-food joints, and gobs of retail shops on merchant laden streets. It was also our town's standby, the go-to place for Friday night dinners, Saturday movie matinees, and liquor-fueled night life. Not that MY family indulged in any of those "costly" hijinks. Heaven forbid. But sometimes it was appropriate and fun to travel even farther and take in a larger metropolis. We would pile into the Oldsmobile station wagon early on a selected Saturday and take off. No food or water graced the pristine interior of the car. And bathroom breaks were for the weak. That was the norm for my family. Contrast that with the car travels my wife and children embarked on years later: multiple bathroom stops, squawking about enough provisions for a two-hour ride, bottles of bottled water galore, crackers, candy, etc. In our day, when we finally arrived at our parking garage destination, my old man would lead us to a familiar cheap diner to freshen up and have a bite to eat from the cafeteria-style food service. No tipping made this my father's favorite eating establishment. But no one became dehydrated or hypoglycemic from our paltry lunches. To be honest, however, my sister and I were allowed a small bag of unshelled peanuts and one square each of white chocolate to salivate on and savor during our afternoon shopping spree. At Big N., pop would stock up on fishing gear and supplies and mom would try on shoes. I would check out science books at Fowler's Dept. store while my sister looked at the dolls in the toy department. We shopped, we bought, we went home late. We drove away hungry and thirsty, as usual. Upon arriving home, mom would hastily prepare supper as we excitedly yammered and fondled our new purchases. I'm sure my friends and their families traveled to "big cities" much as we did. Perhaps they brought refreshments with them and ate dinner at some swanky restaurant in the evening. I don't know. I was never told 'cause I never asked. Nevertheless, to my folks it was always about the end results, not the uncomfortable automobile ride, the discomforts of the present, or even the lack of proper nutrition during the shopping day. It was all about the goods, and saving a buck here and there.

Take a break!

SIXTH GRADE

80

The Slide Show

Sixth grade began with a social studies topic on our western U.S. national parks and historic monuments. I figured it was part of the normal curriculum and it was, sort of. After a few days spent enumerating the many scenic and well-known locations across the U.S.A., found mostly in the western states, our teacher, Mrs. O., brought in a special guest. He was the father of a set of painfully shy but exceedingly bright fraternal twin girls in my class. Mr. P. was a college business professor and recently returned from an extended summer hiatus with his family, having visited a panoply of the very places we were currently studying. Coincidence? I think not. I'm sure Mrs. O. had it all planned out in advance. It wasn't just providence that he arrived with boxes of slides, his own projector (that worked), and index cards to glance at for a prepared talk. The entire morning was devoted to his very detailed and prolonged dog-and-pony show. He and his family had a Winnebago motor home and used it to traverse the country while photographing and noting the flora, fauna, and countryside. We were treated to a carefully choreographed and catalogued "Parks" trip out west, during the summer of 1970. It's funny how his daughters never said boo about the vacation. They hardly spoke at all, however. Nevertheless, we all knew how insanely smart they were and left them alone. No teasing, no nothing. Other sixth grade classes had been invited to our room for that morning session on parks and recreation. Mr. P. covered Mount Rushmore, Yosemite, Yellowstone, etc., to a standing room only crowd in a darkened classroom. He wrapped things up by lunchtime and packed up to go. Everyone clapped and stared at his beaming daughters. As a professor he knew how to lecture and we learned plenty that morn. The next day Mrs. O. had each student pick a federal/national/state parkland or nature preserve to research and write about. I chose Zion National Park, located in southwestern Utah. You know, the one with the huge, squarish-looking bare mountain formations. Mr. P. had described it well and I had an easy time cribbing and paraphrasing his knowledge for my own project. Although unnecessary, I completed it with a detailed hand-drawn landscape on the front cover. Enthusiastically, I told my folks about the traveling, the luxurious motor coach, and the fun times Mr. P. and his family had "discovering" America. My nonplussed father frowned and remarked that OUR family would once again be pop-up camping next summer at Hammonasset Beach State Park, in Connecticut; OUR old faithful.

81

Who Dat Fast Boy?

As I have previously mentioned, yes, I was a rather nimble juvenile athlete. And by sixth grade I even started to fill out a bit. And not in the gut, but in the pectoral and shoulder regions. Not bad for prepuberty. Anyway, there I was, feeling good about myself, psychologically and physically. Though not a classic jock – I was too smart – I nonetheless held my own among my sporty peers, in gym class and on the playground. And thanks to lots of table tennis practice with my dad, on our own table in the basement, using a professional model Stiga laminated wooden blade with Yasaka Mark V rubber, and Halex three-star balls, I began to trounce all comers on the beat-up ping pong table in the boy's locker room. Also, the varsity tennis coach had heard about me and looked forward to my continued improvement on the court. The only thing that chafed me was the discrete discrimination I felt from the gym teachers I had had thus far. I could out sprint the future quarterbacks and running backs. I even excelled at dodgeball when played in gym class and in the same gymnasium during rainy recess periods against much older kids. Although my phys ed grades finally accurately reflected my physical abilities, after my mother's notorious blowup with a certain P.E. teacher, the animosity toward me on indoor and outdoor playing fields was palpable, at least to me. Gym teachers/coaches seemed confused. To their small-minded thinking, I appeared to be the token "black" kid who was congratulated on the one hand but overlooked and dissed on the other. I felt the undercurrents of racism and underlying hatred but could not alter the situation. Of course my "funny sounding" surname, and parents who spoke with an accent, only further stigmatized and stereotyped me in their eyes. It was a hopeless and helpless feeling realizing that I would never be one of *them*. I was born in America, dammit! It frequently made me frustrated and angry, being dealt with in this way. But once or twice my mom did remind me that my ancient Christian Orthodox Estonian ancestors were originally from the eastern Caucasus mountain region. Technically, that made me a Caucasian. What did that make the bigoted local yokels in my adopted village and high school? If I was "white," what were they?

82

B.H. and Bad Math

Not BAD meth, but BAD math! Jeepers creepers. After
being waylaid by "new math" in first grade, taught by that
wigged out and bitchy Mrs. H., I sincerely thought I was
over the hump, numerically speaking. Well I wasn't. I
understood second through fifth grade arithmetic and
accumulated top grades, but I was thoroughly ambushed
by sixth grade mathematics. And B.H., a certain student
in my class that year, did not make things any easier for
me, nor did the stately teacher Mrs. O. The math that year
was not really new, but tried-and-true concepts that were
new to me and my classmates. But why was I so stymied?
I was supposedly "smart." Why didn't I understand and
easily master some of those abstract ideas while most of the
class did? Was it B.H.'s fault? Let's digress for a minute.
Every time old Mrs. O. would open with a new math
topic, B.H. would begin squirming in his seat and start
acting up. Perhaps he despised math as much as I did and
that was his coping mechanism? Before we got to our first
problem trying to solve powers, such as 2 squared or 3
cubed, Mrs. O. would glare at B.H. and he knew what that
meant: a five-minute time-out session in the hallway

outside the classroom. So just as I was trying to concentrate and comprehend the logic behind cubes and difficult word problems, there would be B.H., with his shirt off, writhing, showcasing a wide assortment of silly faces and, gesticulating in front of the glass window of the class door, making all of us inside laugh. We couldn't help ourselves. He was a riot. Mrs. O. would turn to the door and pretend to rush toward it. B.H. would stop the monkeyshines but then restart them when she wasn't looking. My already weak math brain couldn't learn in that halting and chaotic environment. I blamed it all on B.H. but it was actually MY lack of reasoning ability that sunk me that year. Mrs. O. announced that later in the school year, certain students would begin learning "high math" from Mrs. P. next door, another sixth grade teacher. My pride and ego were already suffering greatly. I just had to get into THAT coveted class, at least to get my pop off my back. I redoubled my efforts in class, did not look at B.H.'s antics at the door, and memorized that torpid and nonsensical arithmetic at long last. However, my fingernails took a beating for a few tense months as I grappled with that topic. Nevertheless, I was selected to the "high math" group and quickly realized that I didn't belong there. The once-a-week class was brutal. I was angry at myself for not getting "it" like others did. What was wrong with me? I was a fake, a fraud. My lack of number skills was fully exposed in that math class. I was barely in the A minus range when the year ended but even that was a generous grade for me. I was a phony and both Mrs. O. and Mrs. P. knew it. I was downgraded behind closed doors and started seventh grade in regular instead of eighth grade "advanced math." My father couldn't believe it and was outraged at me. I feigned disappointment but was relieved at the same time. I think my old man also knew that numerology was not my strong suit and backed off somewhat. Although to be fair, in ninth grade algebra, a few years in the future, I suddenly understood math; it clicked for me and I flourished in that class. Go figure. But at the end of sixth grade I was a beaten foe and knew that my *smart* friends would leave me behind a bit as they advanced mathematically and I didn't. And B.H.? He went on to BOCES, so I could not blame him anymore for my mathematical ineptitude. I hated math then, and still do, although I received an A in calculus in pharmacy college; both semesters. What the hell?

83

I Hate to Read

That's a very strong sentiment to have, especially coming from an author; well, a comedic impresario that can put down a few funny words on paper without grammatically stumbling too much. But is it really true? Let's find out. Sixth grade had already begun. Our teacher, statuesque and matronly Mrs. O., quickly singled out ten students in the class and told us to stay during lunch, to have an important meeting with her. I had no clue what this was about. She had her poker face on. First of all, how did she know anything about us, and more importantly, what about lunch? Obviously, the fifth grade teachers had colluded and tattled on us; spilled the beans, so to speak. Mrs. O. now had all ten of we "special" sixth graders in her room. She told us not to worry, she would provide the food. Good, lunch was saved. We met with her that noon, *noshed* on the delicious non cafeteria pizza which she had bought, and listened intently to a curious program she described. We would be meeting weekly with another teacher named Mrs. G., in our former elementary school building, to learn how to speed-read in an hourly session. We were told it was an "experimental" initiative originally spearheaded by president JFK to catch up to those smart-alecky Soviets. That educational plan had finally made its way to our "backwater" village and high school. Speed-reading? I thought I already breezed through the written word and had decent memory, but the word "experimental" sounded downright scary and neat at the same time. I was anxiously all in but were we going to be graded for it? No one said anything about that. I told my parents and they both shrugged. "How hard could it be? You already know how to read," chuckled my pop. I found out that Friday. We "chosen ones" arrived at school, took off our coats, said the Pledge of Allegiance, waited for attendance to be taken, put our coats back on and dutifully left our classroom to begin the ten-minute climb up to the elementary school at the top of the hill. It was familiar territory and terrain. We had all just left there a few years past. We walked up, all the while teasing each other and talking with much bravado. It was a privilege to leave school unattended and be trusted like that. Our group was composed of six girls and four boys; we had all known each other since kindergarten. We were all "originals" (not transfer students) and had no secrets from each other. No "experiment" was going to bushwhack us! We found the place after walking down familiar hallways that now looked narrow. Everything appeared to be smaller than I had remembered. We squeezed into the tiny room and took seats behind long tables. Mrs. G. was smiling and cackling like a hen that had just found a worm. She handed out smelly, mimeographed answer-type papers to us. The front of the room had a large screen and a noisy, space-age looking projector that was percolating behind us. We were ready. Ready for what? We did have sharpened No 2 pencils just in case of trouble, however. And the trouble soon began. The lights were doused and the blinds lowered. We sat there looking like baby owls, eyes wide open and heads swiveling from side to side. Mrs. G. quickly told us what would happen. A series of sentences would appear on the screen from left to right at a certain velocity. After the barrage of words was complete, the lights would come on and we would answer questions about the short story that we had been forced to consume. It sounded simple, even easy. That first Friday my classmates and I killed it. We got all the answers right; 100 percent. As we swaggered back to the high school I smugly thought that I was a fast reader. What a chump I was. Mrs. G. had set us up, but good. Very carefully, on ensuing Fridays, she would slowly ratchet up the *speed* of the verbage spilled onto the screen. We cocky clods knew it but no one complained. Still 100 percent right answers, baby! This went on for a few months and then gradually and insidiously our test scores started to falter and fall. It got to the point that by December our eyes were merely flailing at the blurry words dancing and whizzing by us on that darn screen. We were hooked like addicts and had to futilely keep proving that we could "do it," but quietly started to complain among ourselves. Mrs. G. persevered and ignored our simmering outrage. I thought of that popular slogan on TV at the time: Reading is FUNdamental. In her class it was just mental. Reading and comprehension were becoming chores, hardships and not pleasurable at all. The title of the class was so apropos: speed-reading. It's as if we were HIGH on speed while reading. Then one spring Friday Mrs. G. stopped speeding. She cranked the speed-gun projector just a few ticks lower and guess what happened? We all aced the story. She beamed, we were just relieved to get good scores again. She then blurted out that we had all passed the "experiment;" we could now read faster and understand content better than our classmates, maybe even compete with those pesky Russians. And as a bonus the test results would not count toward our English grade. We sighed in relief, hopefully no one had relieved himself/herself after all that tension was released. The course had ended on a positive note and we were finished. But, ironically, here is what transpired later in my life: I became a voracious reader and could devour obscene quantities of print in big bites, and with great recall. It proved useful in high school, pharmacy college and dental school. However, I could not slow down. Now I always had to read fast. I knew no other way. Consequently, I often missed the nuances and emotionality in novels. I no longer loved to read. The pleasure of sitting down and enjoying a good book was now lost on me. I thought that perhaps my nervous disposition and endless, dry, science/medical exposure had ruined me but heard through the grapevine that we ten guinea pigs were similarly affected later in life. We all suffered the same fate. To this day I read expeditiously; I hate it. I wonder if that experimental reading class is still taught to select sixth graders in my old school. I suppose we former *zippy* students had indeed proved the hypothesis correct and hopefully surpassed those damn Commies, although at the cost of our "reading" souls.

84

Joining a Cult?

It's every parent's worst nightmare, unless she/he also belonged or belongs to one. Cub Scouts, Brownies, Scientology, The Smokey Bear Association? Yes, our entire class willingly gave Mrs. O. the required nominal monies, which she sent in, and waited patiently to receive bronze-colored badges, certificates of membership, patches, and other trinkets denoting allegiance to fighting forest fires. Hurray for Smokey the Bear! However, were we coerced to join up? The herd mentality? Sure it was a *cool* organization but I don't remember any student objecting to it, not one. We and our folks implicitly trusted the school, the curriculum taught, the teachers, and Mrs. O. But what if Smokey had been bogus, a nefarious bum, full of mischief and sexual misconduct? Would we have known? Was my school steering our porous minds in the "right" directions? It seemed like I waited forever to get my coveted and "officially" signed goods from that *bear*. We opened our packages, proudly displayed the paraphernalia, and exalted in belonging to something so noble. However, I wondered if the indoctrinated Hitler Youth of 1920s Nazi Germany felt the same, with their stinkin' badges and armbands? Were we on a similar slippery slope? We even had a short topic on fire prevention. I may seem openly hostile, slightly paranoid and sensitive about being a "joiner" but that attitude has prevailed throughout my life. I never spliced with a fraternity or sorority while in two professional colleges, nor am I currently a Freemason, a Rotarian, a Mormon, or a Hare Krishna. Nevertheless, I do belong to national and state dental societies, the United States Tennis Association, and the United States Association of Track and Field. Hopefully MY *cults* don't count. Hopefully they haven't brainwashed me into doing something awful without consciously knowing about it. And I still remember how to put out a fire when done camping. Oh, my. Thanks Smokey, I think.

85

Simon Says

What do you do when a classroom of antsy children
suddenly becomes unmanageable? And what if that unruly
class "feeling" cannot easily be tamed? As a veteran and
savvy teacher, do you send them all to the principal's office
for a reprimand? Do you line the halls with them for a
time-out? Or do you drop what you are trying to teach the
boisterous bunch and play Simon Says? Well, smart and
seasoned Mrs. O. always chose the latter, to get our
adrenaline used up in a hurry and then to continue
lecturing. You all know the game, right? A person is
selected to lead the group. Everyone stands and the leader
rapidly implores the gathering to copy her/his often zany
poses by saying: "Simon Says Do This." If the orator
merely shouts out "Do This" and catches some overzealous
students copying the stance, then they lose and have to sit
down. The often raucous and quick tempo, sanctioned,
monkeyshines proceed until there is one child standing.
Then she/he gets the honor of being the new leader and
tries to stump the classroom participants with her/his
unique cadence, weird positions and guile. The whole
episode to discharge our overheated batteries took less than

ten minutes with a few leaders getting us exhausted, ready to simmer down, and able to learn again. I usually did well and became the leader multiple times during the school year whenever Mrs. O. sought to calm us down in a hurry. She was one clever teacher. An aside: Although VERY old at this point, Mrs. O. took it upon herself to phone my office in 2010 and spoke at length to my office receptionist. I didn't know she had called until my receptionist relayed the conversation to me. For some reason, she did not want to speak to me personally but fondly remembered me and gushed at my "success" as a dentist. Good ole' Mrs. O. R.I.P.

86

Back Stabber

Literally, not figuratively. Well not really stabbed, but punched hard nonetheless. P.R., my dubious former best friend from kindergarten, somehow kept passing and ended up in the sixth grade, in the room right next to mine. We did not interact and avoided each other through the whole school year. So I was shocked when, quite suddenly and much to my disdain, he attacked me from behind one day on the way back into our respective rooms after recess. It was only a punch but I could not retaliate because he quickly ducked into his classroom and I went into mine. Again, this unprovoked and biased physical abuse brought back many unsettling memories of our time in first grade, when he would routinely pummel me at the bus stop in the mornings. It wasn't the pain of the punch that got to me but the fear and paranoia associated with it. He knew I would not fight back and probably gloated about his domination over an inferior male, someone whom he had "conquered" before. Sure, there were student witnesses but since I stoically took it without a whimper, they assumed that it was part of some consensual ongoing altercation. I didn't say a word to anyone. Short of walking down the hall backwards so I could see him approaching, there was little I could do. He was sneaky that way. Finally, I had enough and surreptitiously enlisted the assistance of three close friends from my class. I explained the situation to them and beseeched them to help me. All three liked me well enough to go to the principal's office should they get caught and they agreed to ambush the ambusher. It all went down on a Monday. Same hallway, same walk back to class, only this time I had eyes in the back of my head: my three pals were stealthily watching for him. Right on cue, he ran for me out of nowhere but was intercepted and seized by my buddies. L. J., my tall friend who had failed a grade, quickly figured out my plight and joined in the melee. It wasn't much really. I turned and saw a frightened P.R., in the grip of my chums, staring at me in bewilderment. They each in turn socked him hard in the back and sat his ass down on the drinking fountain in the hallway and turned on the water. I didn't do a thing but his power over me instantly dissipated. He burst off that fountain, yelled profanities in our direction, and ran down to the nurse's station to get a new pair of pants. S.M., F.D., M.L., and L.J. had saved me. They were busy laughing in the hall while I was seriously thanking them in turn. The surrounding student witnesses did not squeal and NO one got in trouble.

However, P.R. never touched me again. That episode makes it sound like I was the class wimp. Not true. I was very athletic and the de facto class clown, with a sharp wit. That personality trait alone seemed to keep unsavory characters away from me. Most of my peers, boys and girls, thought highly of me, from what I had heard. However, sometimes you had to hit back when set upon. You just had to, to send a message of respect. I just wasn't the violent type. I would continue to slay my enemies with my tongue, through high school and beyond. Although maybe I should have thrown a few haymakers at P.R. when he was pinned down and vulnerable that day, long ago. I bet it would have felt good.

87

Maxie's

It was a stalwart institution and locally famous landmark
all right. A hotbed of young students circled that joint in
the mornings, at noon and after school let out. I know, I
know, it was only a Gulf gasoline station, just down the hill
from the school, across the bridges, and owned by the
Maxie family. But it functioned as the sugary hub for all
we underaged kids. A welcome wagon full of sweet treats
to purchase. It was always Halloween at Maxie's. There
was penny candy, bubblegum, hot balls, taffy, ice cream,
popsicles, etc. All cheap stuff, chock full of cyclamates and
tasty too. Old man "Maxie" himself sold it all, and also
gasoline. Maybe even a car repair thrown in as needed.
However, most of the station's income looked as though it
came straight from the steady stream of adolescents
shuffling in and out of that small, white concrete room,
year-round. Of course the local supermarkets and other
stores in town carried the same delicious garbage, but they
were farther from the school. Plus Maxie's had a certain
moxie reputation. It was a *cool* place. What child
WOULDN'T want to be associated with it? I confess to
eating my fair share of grape-flavored popsicles on the way

home from the village pool during the summers but I never stopped in to grab a small snack during the school year. I always had a few jingling coins in my pocket but wasn't tempted to stop for a treat. I'm not sure why. My parents would never have known one way or the other. Nevertheless, by sixth grade a few enterprising students in my class would load up at Maxie's and then sell the school-banned substances for a profit. You know, a penny here, a penny there. Hey, business is business. But it was illegal on school grounds; chewing gum and eating candy in class were no-nos. So what, the infractions were many but the laws were not enforced. That's how things went. By seventh grade, when students were allowed to go off school property for lunch, entrepreneurial seventh graders would run down to Maxie's with student orders and then discretely unload and sell their wares in bathrooms, in darkened hallways and behind teachers' backs. It was all in good fun, however. No one really got into trouble and even I spent a few nickels on that artificially sweetened shit. Many was the time when I witnessed purple gumballs flying across the classroom and then a few dimes come whizzing over our heads, going in the opposite direction. Only the boys were involved in this brazen behavior. Girls would also satisfy their sweet tooth, albeit discretely, and without the swag attached. By eighth grade, the *candy fad* was over for we middle-schoolers. Nonetheless, "Maxie" supplied the next generation coming up behind us, and the next, etc. He kept pumping students full of profitable junk while pumping gas in their parents' cars. But as our childlike confection addiction waned, new forms of oral gratification arouse, namely nicotine agents. Smokes and chewing tobacco, also sold at Maxie's, reared their ugly heads by eighth grade. Minors were forbidden to buy cigarettes but somehow tobacco products insidiously trickled into our school and supplanted saccharin as the new *Kool* fixation. One vice down, another in its place. Lots of the ladies got snookered by that new, nasty habit, as well. Fortunately, I never became hooked on either. Just lucky, I guess.

88

Gilligan's Daughter?

At midyear, a female transfer student appeared in our class. That was odd in itself. But when her name was announced to us by Mrs. O., we took little notice. She was from Los Angeles and looked the part; leather leggings, beads on her leather clothing, wrist jewelry, headbands, scarves, and a fringed purse. S. Victor Tallarico (Steven Tyler) of Aerosmith would have been proud of her getup. She told us she was Hawaiian in origin. That would explain her Polynesian-type facial features and skin tone. We boys still took no real notice until she blurted out who her father was, well, adoptive father that is. We stood and stared at her after that revelation. Gilligan, from *Gilligan's Island* fame was her dad? That's what she said. And that's how I heard it. It seemed that a parental split caused her mother, brother and she to end up living in the family's summer playland, in a hamlet outside our village. Her new home was replete with real lions, tigers and bears, etc. She had proof; she showed us pictures. The fully staffed ranch was not some local delipidated farm but a multimillion-dollar spread, hidden away from prying eyes on some unmarked, deserted back road. She was there because of marital discord on her mother's part and didn't appreciate being away from southern California, her toney lifestyle and trendy friends. I can only imagine how some of our *home gurls* felt, dressed in OshKosh denim overalls and with butchered haircuts. I'm sure they gave her the once-over and probably wanted to literally strangle that beautiful, slightly pretentious and rich bitch, on the spot. She was so exotic looking and seemed to glide effortlessly when she walked. We boys were enthralled. She was *smart* and a "gifted" artist as well. Damn, she had it all. I was no longer the only "artist" in the class, or the smart guy with funny retorts. She also had a wicked sense of humor. I hated transfer students. Just kidding. We had a few things in common and liked to draw together, and to study butterflies. But she always had her guard up and never revealed her true self, at least not to me. We evolved into acquaintances at best. The scholastic year ended and none from my class had ever been invited to her place for any kind of get-together. I thought she would have loved to show off her animals, wealth, and privilege to we pikers, but it never happened. I do remember her fifth grade brother, whom she said was biologically Gilligan's son, being mercilessly teased for having long hair. California must have been way ahead of we "farmers;" we didn't grow our hair out until the middle seventies. The Beatnik movement was slow to catch on with the crew-cut rednecks in our area. Anyway, Julie and her brother blended in as best they could and lasted one more school year before suddenly disappearing. I have tried to look her up on the Internet, but to no avail. I believed her story and lineage back then. Today, I'm not so sure. Was she really Bob Denver's adopted daughter? Were they estranged? I would like to know.

89

Ichabod Crane

What a peculiar sounding name, right? A name we all grew up with from our youth because of the spooky, mysterious and unresolved disappearance of the main character in the widely read book *The Legend of Sleepy Hollow* by Washington Irving. The amusing and provocative protagonist's name heralded a certain mockery, whimsy and curiosity. Well, there is also a high school named Ichabod Crane and it sits in the Catskills, near where Irving supposedly based many of his seminal stories on, including *Rip Van Winkle*, etc. This particular high school was a thorn in my derriere. It seemed that every winter season, when it came to school closings, it was right up there at the number one position for total number of times shuttered. It was downright comical. My sister and I would silently listen to the only station with a decent reception in our hilly geographical area, WGY AM radio, for its weather and school closing reports on snowy days, wishing for a snow day, but all for naught. We would cynically predict and then laugh out loud whenever Ichabod Crane was announced. Our school was rarely, if ever mentioned. A three-foot overnight dump of snow?

No problem. We couldn't go out to make snowmen, snow forts or go sledding. WE had to *schlep* to school! Yet Ichabod Crane must have gotten it worse, I guessed. Its frequent closure was also the running joke in my school. "Everyone" knew that it was ALWAYS closed in the wintertime. Sometimes it was the ONLY school on the closed list. Why? How many allotted *snow days* did it have? My sister and I imagined it to be on some craggy mountaintop or in a deep ravine where snowy blizzards obliterated it on a regular basis while the rest of us were spared. My folks didn't know exactly where it was; somewhere in the deep Catskills they would say. This went on all through my elementary and high school educational tenure. Fast forward to the early 1990s: My grown sister and her family moved to a newly built (by my father and grandfather, who else?) home in the Catskills and I, my wife and young children were invited for an opulent reception dinner at their new digs. The first hour of the drive was uneventful, our minivan successfully traversed the many twists and turns and steep inclines common for that area. It was a pleasant summer's day as I was mindlessly driving along and happened to glance over to my left during a long stretch of flat highway. I looked, then stared, then violently jerked our minivan onto the right shoulder and braked hard in a sliding skid before stopping. My dozing wife and napping kids were terrified. What was it? A deer? A fox? A woodchuck or possum in the road? I just sat there speechless and horror-stricken, pointing to the left. My wife recovered enough to read the name on the campus building across the road: Ichabod Crane High School. My bane, my nemesis, was finally revealed to me. My visually impaired toddler son could not see it but my daughter could, and she described it quite poignantly to us all. My family had heard of the woeful tales about this school. They knew it was my "sworn enemy." Then everyone in the car, including my son, cracked up. I chuckled softly as I peered around at the bland surroundings. There were no mountaintops, no ditches, no gullies, no gulches. It was flat land. Did it snow harder here than in the rest of our state? Were the people here wimps or easily distressed lawn gnomes? What made this modern looking high school so vulnerable to the snowflake? Anyway, my sister's house was rather close by, in the next town over, and we arrived there shortly thereafter. I had a zillion questions for her about THAT high school. She remembered it as well but could not answer any of my futile queries. However, she did add that the recent winter at her new place was about the same as the ones we had at our parental home, no harsher, no milder. But to be fair, she had only been through one winter thus far. And Ichabod Crane had only closed twelve times, so she really could not judge that well. I was mystified then and still am to this day. Much later, my grown son and I had the opportunity and pleasure of competing in official USATF track and field events together, different age groups of course, at Ichabod Crane High School in the summers. Its track was reasonably good, as was the javelin vector. Those days were often warm, sunny and free of snow. However, NO one ever gave me a rational and satisfactory explanation as to the amount of snow closures that the school employed, because it was still going on! Fifty-plus years later and the mystery of Ichabod Crane continues....

90

Off the Hook

As a converted city boy my father fell in love with hikin', huntin' and fishin' in his new country town. Although a professor and learned man, he loved *manly* pursuits outside of academia. Nobody would ever accuse him of being a stuff-shirted bookworm. Tagging along with him as he was sighting his 30-06 hunting rifle on hapless woodchucks before deer hunting season, or investigating white tail deer trails on state land during hikes, brought us closer together. You know there is always that father-son relationship thing, be it antagonistic, synergistic or a combo of both. It can get complicated. But there was one leisurely summer activity that was his and my favorite: fishing. Our go-to spot was Spring Lake, a tiny, DEC-protected body of water just outside our village, and surrounded by farmland. There was one residence on the shore at the north end and it belonged to our county sheriff: "Stretch." His son E. was in my class. S.G., a "rare" female friend of mine, lived up a dirt road, also in close proximity to that body of water. Everyone that went fishing or boating there knew that the sheriff could he home watching the lake, so no one wantonly misbehaved, threw out trash, started fires, etc. It was a relatively "safe" lake, G-rated, and fun for the entire family. Most of the time we would be alone, just my father and me, either casting from shore or from our small aluminum water craft. Sometimes my whole family went for a day's outing, punting along in the overcrowded boat, trying to fish in between heads and shoulders that were in the way. Once in a while my Grandpa Pete would tag along. But he was no fisherman; he had no patience. Like everything else in his *structured* life, he treated fishing like a job: you put the worm on the hook, cast out the line, and caught a fish. When the last part failed to materialize in a timely manner, he became agitated and cranky. He rarely went with us, however, and stayed home to do "something constructive." The lake was full of pickerel, bluegill and pumpkinseed sunfish, bullheads, walleyes, and bass. I had that lake memorized and knew where all those slippery, scaled animals lived. The bass preferred the submerged logs in shallow water. Pickerel liked to jump out in ambush from reedy shore banks, etc. Sunfish were always around but even they sometimes took a day or two off. I didn't care if we went home empty-handed because I got to spend quality time with my pop. Who cared about the fish, anyway? I won't bore you with fishing details like the day I speared a bullhead with a trident-tipped broom handle, or the time we wisely waited out a storm after a day of windy angling, while tying the boat to the top of our station wagon. We left when the weather improved and were amazed at the damage caused by a rare twister that had touched down near our village. Anyhow, the gist of this story was to discuss my feelings while being in that dinghy with my father. Why the significance? Well, I was mired in a rowboat on a puny lake where locals usually got drunk and fished. Big deal, right? But it was to me. Because there was my idol, my drill sergeant, my harshest critic, sitting a mere four feet away from me and seemingly relaxed and placid. And he didn't drink any alcohol while onboard. Only water. We would talk about fishing, about life, philosophy, current events in the news, etc. He was a smart man and knew a lot about everything. We had joyful and deep conversations out there. His son (me) was his fishing buddy, not a whipping boy, not a GPA average, not a kid who could never pass muster. We were "equals" in that tub, at least until sundown made us pack it in, and our shadows chased us home. I remember and cherish those brief hours I spent alone with him, musing about the universe and the meaning of life. I hated to continually disappoint him but I viewed myself as an imperfect and inferior child. He let that slide while on the water and I was grateful. Years later, as both a professionally and financially successful dentist, not to mention a competitive tennis player and track and field athlete, my mother once casually mentioned to me that my father was very proud of his only son. Me? Really? Since when? Did he have a stroke or something? WTF? All my adult life I thought I was still under the gun, his gun. Had it all been a clever and long running ruse on his part to keep my momentum moving in the right direction? Was he really that psychologically insightful about raising offspring? But had he ALWAYS been proud of me, or only now that I had surpassed him academically, athletically and monetarily? I don't know and probably never will. Perhaps my father had always been a doting, loving and encouraging parent in his mind and in my young life, but I squandered his positive overtures and instead "heard" a twisted and totally different tune from him. Maybe I was the cynical, ungrateful, and recalcitrant minor who was WAY too sensitive in dealing with his withering but justified criticisms of me? Maybe all of the above? As an old-timer myself now, I had let my old man off the hook years ago but I don't think he realized that he was ever on it. And our tenuous relationship improved greatly as I grew older; he selflessly helped my family and me for years and I was grateful. Now back to the past: Seventh grade would be starting in the fall and I was ready to continue. I had no choice but to live up to new expectations and my future.

91

The Schwinn Twins

Before I was gifted my old man's 1959 Campagnolo
derailleur systemed, Raleigh ten-speed, I was fortunate
enough to own an expensive, genuine, golden Schwinn
five-speed. The original one, made in the U.S.A., not the
Chinese knockoff, which came years later. My sister,
though a first grader, also had a new, blue Schwinn, but
was not allowed to follow me down to Clinton Street to
ride. She could only cycle her bike on our short, dead-end
street until she was a little older. I had permission to cruise
down the steep hill to our old haunts, on that gorgeous,
tree-lined, wide street, and ride to my heart's content. I
lived two minutes away and it still felt like home. There
was very light traffic, if any, on it and I knew most
everyone there. It was as if I had never left that cloistered
and unique community. I no longer brought my butterfly
net in tow but still stopped in regularly to "talk shop" with
old Dr. R., my entomological *patron saint*. I was doing
most of my insect collecting at home now and left the
widows of Clinton Street and their backyards alone.
Maybe I was growing up somewhat? Perhaps. Riding my
Schwinn was special, though. It was a fine bike, heavy,

solid, and reliable. My chain never came off, the pedals did not rust and the steering was tight. I never even had a flat tire. It was one sweet bicycle, with a generator powered headlight and red tail lamp, as well. One early summer day, after I had obtained consent from my mom to ride, and effectively slipped out from the grasp of my project-obsessed Grandpa Pete, I noticed another rider at the far end of the street. I had not seen this person on MY turf before. I rode toward the *rogue* rider, both of us stopping for an introduction in the middle of the macadam coated roadway. Wait, I knew her, she was a year older than me in school and kind of an acknowledged and very intelligent tomboy, complete with a butch haircut and glasses. And she was sitting on a boy's, five-speed, white Schwinn! How cool was that? Our respective fathers were college professors and we sort of knew about each other, so all was *kosher* at our initial meeting. We decided to loosely pick favorite times of the week to meet and ride together. Sometimes we rode solo, nothing was definite or strictly preplanned. We didn't phone each other for real dates. Plus sometimes I would park my pedaled steed behind the First Presbyterian church or next to Mr. Wall's house on Wooley Street and steal down to the brook for a quick look-see. We probably missed each other on some days. She lived on High Street, about ten minutes away, but also valued the expanse and riding pleasure of Clinton Street. We were the Schwinn twins that summer and had fun racing each other, while shifting gears, up and down that beautiful boulevard. But nothing lasts forever as I graduated to my hand-me-down ten-speed Raleigh shortly thereafter, and I suppose she upgraded as well. We saw each other sporadically in school the following fall but had nothing in common and our riding friendship effectively faded. There had been no sexual sparks between us in the boy-meets-girl department either. Plus she was an avowed lesbian, as I later learned, but who knew what that even meant in those ignorant days? It makes sense now as I examine our past interactions. Nevertheless, I miss those carefree Schwinn days of yesteryear, and miss her as well.

92

The Brook

My dear friend, my teacher, my surrogate parent. That's how I felt about my special bond with that seemingly insignificant, shallow, narrow stream, running behind the huge Victorian homes on Clinton Street, on the western fringes of my village. It ran from a small, protected reservoir to the north, meandered south through town, and eventually trickled into the West Branch of the Delaware River just past Elm Street, near the center of our community. I was introduced to that particular brook by my nature loving mother, during long walks along Clinton Street, our home road. I instantly became mesmerized by the beauty and solitude of that little tributary, lined with small pools filled with minnows, and miniature eddies swirling near the edges. Living across the quiet street made it easy to get to, and once I befriended all the kindly widows with my boyish charm, it became a summer refuge for me and all my naturalistic proclivities. Although only six years old, I was granted permission to trespass on most properties that abutted that magical rivulet to do my thing. What was my thing? Why, to explore, discover and catch salamanders, mudpuppies and other slimy, aquatic and buggy critters. Blissfully flipping rocks at the water margins kept me occupied for hours and often yielded northern two-lined salamanders in droves. Once in a while a blue-spotted salamander or totally aquatic mudpuppy would grace my bucket after being skillfully caught in my net. Those denizens of the drink would be kept as "pets" for short time periods and then let go. I had nets, sieves, old spaghetti strainers, buckets, boots, etc. Although not a Boy Scout, Cub Scout, Webeloe, or even a Brownie, I was always prepared for my adventurous *collecting* excursions. Frogs, toads, water naiads (dragonfly nymphs), grubs, crayfish, snakes, fishing spiders, water boatmen, backswimmers, etc., were also on my hit list. As I grew older I found new entrances and egresses to that wondrous bourn. Even after moving to my new home, I remained only five minutes away. I would ease down the hill, wave to Mr. Wall, carefully walk behind his tall pines bordering Wooley Street, and then descend a few steps into "my" remarkable world. If a butterfly chanced to come by for a muddy sip, it was usually caught to add to my growing collection, or just to examine. But on one dreary summer day in 1971, after an unforecast, twenty-four-hour rainy deluge, the friendly and babbling brook turned into a belligerent and brutal beast, flooding our settlement with a foot or more of muddy water inundating Main, Clinton and Elm streets. It was a horrible catastrophe for an unprepared populace. It was all because one log had jammed up against a bridge abutment and effectively plugged the downstream flow of the silty water. But to be fair, other local creeks and nearby rivers also rose and contributed to the watery debacle. Mom and I were ignorant as we walked down our hill the next day to go shopping and were promptly stopped by a volunteer fireman and told to return home. Glancing behind me I saw tadpoles and fingerling trout helplessly splashing about on rain soaked lawns. What a mess. We trudged back to our house on our hilly street and turned on the local AM radio news. Yes, the reports were of a locally devastated village, due to an unforeseen cloudburst and one large tree trunk. But the West Branch of the Delaware also crested high and wouldn't have been able to absorb the extra liquid pumping furiously into it from *my* brook anyway. After the cleanup and drying out of damaged cellars, the townspeople decided that properly widening and dredging ALL local streams was the answer to prevent future watery calamities. Future forays to MY favorite haunt saw changes. My favorite rocks, low lying branches, and curved embankments were now missing. The brook's personality was forever altered; like having a lobotomy. I missed my old friend. However, it had to be done. Many unsuspecting people had lost valuable possessions. The local college president, for instance, suffered a ruined garage and had all his lawn care equipment swept away. He hated to mow anyway, however. But after dredging the bottom and close-shaving its banks, future storms, no matter how vicious, never again caused my little waterway to rise up and terrorize the villagers.

93

Bucolic Living

For all my previous rants and gripes about "surviving" in a dusty, sleepy, and "good-for-nothing" village in the middle of nowhere, I apologize, sort of. Although born in a large, industrialized city, in western New York State and while immersed in it firsthand while on numerous extended summer visits there, it got me thinking about my actual childhood, reared in the "country" instead. It made me realize just how fortunate I had been to be "stuck" in that beautiful and bucolic mudhole in upstate New York. It wasn't much to look at but the fresh air, fresh produce, clean water, open spaces, unlimited access to fields and streams, and freedom from crime punctured city living with an audible pop. It was essentially Mayberry, folks. At least it was in the late sixties and early seventies. Sure, there were petty prejudices and scholastic shenanigans that I dealt with, but in retrospect I wouldn't have wanted it any other way. I loved being raised in the Catskills and I sincerely mean that.

94

A Cautionary Tale

To liberally paraphrase Willy Wonka (the witty Gene Wilder, not that pretentious twit Johnny Depp) as to what happens when a man gets everything he ever wanted: he lives happily ever after. Is that what happened to me? Yes and no. "Be careful what you wish for. There is a price paid for everything in life. And freebies, a free lunch and lady luck are far and few between." Were those three sentences just *wise* axioms to live by or overtly pessimistic diatribes by bitter old men/women who never succeeded in life? I don't know, but please indulge me as I briefly try to explain my adulthood based on my state of being as a grammar school grunt in the following salient sentences: I always felt like an outsider trying to prove myself to a strict and demanding father, grandfather, teachers, classmates, and myself. Being under constant duress, I morphed into a high-strung and stressed out child who bit his fingernails in frustration for not measuring up. Some of it was self-inflicted perfectionism, the rest from unrealistic expectations set up for me at home. Yet to the outside world I was a talented amateur naturalist, athlete, musician, scholar, and wisecracking "foreigner" that made people smile, smirk and occasionally crack up. I was purposely living a "bipolar existence," but then didn't a lot of boys and girls do the same in those days? And adults, too? No one ever bothered to dig deeply into my psyche at that age. No one ever bothered to ask me how I really felt about myself or things in general. But perhaps all those "bad" times that I endured were embellishments and internalized as trauma when in fact they may have been unintentional facets of growing up that everyone went through. It was nothing personal, just business as usual: something called LIFE. I was never willfully abused, either mentally or physically, while growing up. I'm sure other kids had it worse than me. So why did I have thoughts about being so often "victimized?" Those painful moments were fleeting, however, like the butterflies and salamanders I was always chasing. I'm positive other classmates were similarly afflicted but no one discussed such matters back then. At least not openly. With 20/20 hindsight I can now say that those anguishing times that affected my pea brain were not nearly as tragic as I had made them out to be in my mind. Many episodes were comical, some of which you have already read about. This leads me to the last parts of this vignette: I started out as the new kid in town and in my kindergarten class. I did not resemble anyone and had a "weird" last name. However, perhaps because of that angst-ridden beginning, or maybe by happenstance, I started to develop a sense of humor. And I believe it saved me from myself. Not only did many seemingly mundane and daily life events strike me as being funny, I also started to give classmates hilarious commentary and smart-alecky double-talk. I began to use puns, metaphors, innuendos and sarcastic, snide rejoinders during conversations. The class clown was coming to life! Most of my closest buds seemed to enjoy my growing levitous persona and others, even girls, didn't seem to mind at all. This encouraged me to keep joking around, as needed. Green light, baby. Bombs away! But was it a coping mechanism for me, to escape from my imagined dreary and dire existence, regardless of whether that was true or not? Perhaps. Even if it was an escape valve for me, I still made people laugh, even my stoic and stodgy folks. And I greatly enjoyed doing that. Slowly, I became known for my caustic wit and snarky remarks, and by sixth grade I was feeling it. I sneakily loved watching comedies on TV such as Abbott and Costello, The Marx Brothers, The Three Stooges, etc. They became inspirational models to me. I related to them. Sixth grade ended and I was ready to move forward as an athletically inclined, studious student, and as a "comedian." The ensuing years have already been written about by me in my other books, but suffice it to say that most of my infantile dreams and aspirations came true, albeit with the requisite nightmares thrown in. I became a pharmacist and then a financially successful dental specialist yet continue to suffer from over three decades of *Aggravation Saturation*. I even married a *hottie blondie* female that I dreamed I would. And I still play my sports at a high level, in my age group of course. Holy mackerel! Was it all worth it? Was it ALL really my destiny? Probably. I supposedly did all the right things in elementary school thus laying the foundation for my "great" future. I supposedly lived up to my "potential," as forecast by my former teachers, parents and classmates. My retired pharmacist wife and I raised two athletically and academically gifted children who both graduated from tippy top universities, are remarkably well adjusted, and happy in their high-powered chosen professions. Nevertheless, neither one is a dentist, or in any medical field. Smart! Did I bite off more than I could chew? Does it really matter? Does anyone really care? I may have gotten in WAY over my head in life and it continues to sting me in many psychological ways. To reiterate: be careful what you wish for, develop a sense of humor to help deal with life's challenges, and don't become a dentist, although.... My father repeatedly, unequivocally and unwaveringly preached to me and guaranteed that success equals happiness. Furthermore, living in the present and enjoying life's moments were to be eschewed for futuristic planning and worrying at all cost. Well, the future is now my present. Friends, enemies and loved ones have assured me that I finally am a "success." Am I happy now, too?

95

Disclaimer for Former Students

Usually you write disclaimers in a tongue-in-cheek way to obviate yourself from obvious insults, derisive accusations and insinuations. Of course, most of those disclaimers are usually intended for an audience that willingly participated in what was written about. But unless you were homeschooled or truant, elementary school for us *scut-monkeys* was mandatory, compulsory and necessary. This book's often corrosive anecdotal tales, based on real-life victims of education, were intentionally exposed, although they may appear unintentionally malevolent in some parts. It was written mostly in jest. Some levity touched all of we youngsters during those long-ago days and hopefully most of you survived to adulthood, largely unscathed after that forced and often traumatic elementary school upbringing. Read, remember and have fun with the memories, because that's all they are at this point.

96

Last Words

Does anyone's basic character or personality actually transform over time? I mean the person's core values and philosophies regarding life in general? I attend my high school reunions every so often; same people, same problems, same stereotypes, same bullshit. It's as if time stood still for most of us. It's as if we are all still in kindergarten classes, where we were even then primitively jockeying for positions in the student hierarchy of our limited social network. There was the smart one, the dumb one, the shy one, the funny one (me), the mean one, etc. So have any of us changed that much over the decades? We are obviously more educated, worldly, mature, and now sadly decrepit. And have our innate fears and worries subsided, or have they been sublimated into drug addictions and psychological disorders? We had each other pegged from day one when we were five-year-olds but are we nevertheless and forever "elementary" at heart? I don't know, as I reminisce and digress. However, let us hope that at the very least we can still take pleasure in fleeting optimistic feelings and revel in snippets of joy we once possessed in spades. Let's hope.

About the Author

Dr. I. Mayputz (not his real name) graduated with highest honors from high school, from pharmacy college and summa cum laude from dental school. After completing a master's degree in prosthodontics at a then prestigious institution, he embarked on his dental career in private practice. He once briefly toyed with the idea of earning a Ph.D. to become an actual entomologist, but ultimately decided on a dreadfully stressful albeit lucrative career, instead. In addition to being an elite master's athlete, author, naturalist and part-time naturist, he is also known as a caustic wit and provocateur. He wrote this book to entertain family, friends, and any curious sod willing to sneak a peek at the *pee* inside his former elementary school.

For more alleged levity by Dr. I. Mayputz, please read:

Junior High: The Muddle Years

Dental School: A Bizarre Comedy

Pharmacy College: Crazy Daze and Hazy Nites